THE THING IN THE WOODS

MATTHEW W. QUINN

Dea Evey,
Then you for
buying!
[signature] 2
P.S Dont
forget
Kickstarter for
The walking
Wqm

PROLOGUE

LEROY TOLLIVER SAT ON A SMOOTH WOODEN BENCH IN downtown Edington, Georgia across the street from the tall red brick courthouse. He looked up at the big white clock about to strike midnight and pulled a brown paper bag—lighter still than his dark skin—out of the shabby coat he wore even though it was May. He took a swig from the bottle of Mad Dog 2020 wrapped in the paper. The cheap wine stung his tongue like always, but his gag reflex had long adjusted. As he continued drinking, warmth spread from his gut to his hips and throat. This silenced the craving that had been nagging him all day. He grinned. That was the ticket all right.

By his feet, Thompson barked. The skinny, straggly Jack Russell terrier had found him two weeks ago and Leroy liked his company; now he'd spotted something. A shiny green new Cadillac nosed into view from around the courthouse. It pulled to a stop at the red light bisecting the deserted intersection beneath the courthouse. It wasn't one of those SUVs the families who'd been coming from Atlanta the last few years drove—it was too late for them anyway. Probably one of their spoiled brats coming back from a party and hoping his parents were asleep. He hadn't gotten a look at the driver, but it was probably a kid.

He had never driven a car that nice, even when he was on the wagon and working on the Ford plant. Why should some yuppie brat drive that Cadillac when *he* was sleeping in alleys and begging for change? He remembered his own family, before his wife tired of his drinking.

He tilted the bottle all the way up and gulped the last of the alcohol.

"Fuck you!" he spat at the taillights. He threw the bottle at the car. It exploded against the cracked gray asphalt, mere feet from the bumper. The Cadillac jumped forward. The SUV rocketed down the street past the new little park the morons on the county commission thought would bring visitors downtown. It kept going past the old white brick factory block now half-full of retail stores. It didn't slow down for almost a quarter mile.

Tolliver laughed. "Yeah, you run away!" Thompson barked his agreement. "Can't stand your ground like a goddamn man!"

A goddamn *man*. His son Jefferson would be a man now. He hadn't seen the boy for over a decade. He remembered kicking the soccer ball with him in the green grass of Freedom Park in Atlanta one sunny afternoon, the slight breeze keeping the temperature perfect. That night he'd had a bit too much wine and did something he couldn't quite remember. When he sobered up the next day, his wife and son were gone.

Jefferson would be twenty now. Dora was a good woman. She'd wanted the boy to go to college, and she'd squirreled away money in her own name so he couldn't get it. She'd make sure Jefferson would go to a fine school, get a real job. Not a job that'd go away like the Ford plant or that janitor job at the middle school that brought him to Edington before the economy tanked.

Tears trickled down Leroy's dark face into his scraggly, gray-streaked beard. "Hell," he muttered. He didn't have any more Mad Dog to put the memories back where they belonged. Luckily, he had five bucks hidden in his coat. Maybe the gas station down the street had some cheap-ass rotgut for him and a hot dog for Thompson. A hot dog for a dog. He laughed.

He rose and walked over to the hedges behind him where he'd left the shiny shopping cart he'd liberated from the Walmart a few weeks before. He'd stashed his tattered wool blanket there, along with a couple changes of clothes zipped into his seabag. He swore he had another dollar in that pair of blue jeans he'd gotten from the Pentecostal church near Fayetteville Boulevard. If he had six bucks, maybe he could get another hot dog for himself. Shitty meat, but at least it was meat.

He'd wait until he got to a nice quiet alley before he counted his money. That rich brat in the car probably called the cops on him. Best be out of the way, or they'd lock his ass up. Again. And who knew what they'd do to Thompson? The county commission had been cutting the animal shelter's budget too.

The tough rubber of shoe soles scraped against the sidewalk around the corner ahead. Tolliver's head snapped up. Thompson barked. The station was ten minutes' walk away. The police couldn't possibly have come that fast.

His hand sank to his hidden pocketknife. He'd bet it was some gangbanger, some thug with no respect for his elders. If anybody thought he was an easy mark, he'd learn them a lesson right across the fucking face.

Only the intruder wasn't some gangbanger, but a big sheriff's deputy in a starched brown uniform. *Shit.* He couldn't stab

4 MATTHEW W. QUINN

a cop, not unless he wanted to do some *real* hard time. He pulled his hand out of his pocket. If they saw him with his hand down there, they'd shoot his ass dead and act like they were heroes. "Stand Your Ground" and all that cracker bullshit.

He narrowed his eyes as the cop walked his way. It was that fucker Deputy Bowie. The gray-haired cracker had arrested him before, when he'd gotten kicked out of that bar just outside the city limits. He wouldn't be able to talk the deputy into letting him walk. They'd lock him up in a cell without the alcohol that kept him sane. It'd be just like that goddamn hole in the ground in Panama.

Tolliver looked around. Two potential escape routes. To his right, the old metal bridge would take him across the railroad tracks. A klick beyond were some empty shotgun houses he could hide in. Deputy Bowie wouldn't go there without backup, not at night. Too many goddamn gangbangers for that fat fuck. Two klicks left would take him past that greasy little diner with the good leftovers and the sporting goods store to the old bottling plant atop the hill. Break a window, get inside. It's not like anybody would notice, given how badly some past owner's attempt at making it a mini-mall had ended.

"Leroy Tolliver!" Bowie called before he could make the decision. Annoyance was clear on his wide face. "Haven't we been through this before?"

Shit! "Come on, Thompson!" Leroy abandoned the shopping cart and ran, his dog hard at his heels. Maybe he could get around the courthouse annex. Stick to the walls and head up toward Davidson Street. That'd keep him out of sight.

He turned right. They'd think he was going for the bridge. They'd think wrong. "Escape and evade," that's what the Corps had taught him to do in enemy territory. With cops after him, downtown Edington was definitely hostile.

Blue light flashed as a mottled blue and white Edington

Police Department cruiser erupted off a side street to block off the bridge. Thompson slammed into Tolliver's right leg, knocking him forward. A cracker cop who looked barely old enough to shave leaped out from the passenger side and pointed a Taser at him.

"Stop right there!" the policeman demanded.

Tolliver wasn't going to mess with no Taser. He raised his hands. Maybe they'd just give him a lecture about not drinking his ass off. Maybe.

Shoes slapped cement behind him. It was Bowie. He was pinned now, just like he was back in the goddamn Panamanian jungle.

"Leroy Tolliver," Bowie ordered. "Hands behind your back."

Tolliver scowled and obeyed. Merciless metal clamped his wrists together. He was headed for the drunk tank, again.

"Do we take him in?" the younger cop asked.

Bowie shook his head. "Maybe last week. It's been too long. He's getting hungry."

Tolliver's head snapped up, eyes wary. Who the hell was "He" and why was "He" hungry?

The younger cop looked at him, eyes wide and fearful. "Really?"

"Quinn, don't be a pussy. Nobody'll miss this wino."

Son of a bitch! The cops were going to murder him!

Tolliver leaped forward, shouldered aside the younger cop, and rushed down the street. He'd get up the bridge. Someone up there'd help him get those cuffs off. Then he'd hide in the woods for the rest of the night. These pigs wouldn't dare pull this shit in the daylight hours and—

Something stabbed him in the lower back near the scars Noriega's shrapnel had left. Pain flashed the length of his body. His arms and legs stopped working. Somewhere Thompson barked frantically. Tolliver pitched forward face-first into the sidewalk. The gray cement rushed up to strike him in the face and he couldn't even move his arms to cushion the blow.

————

THE ROUGH WOOD of what felt like a goddamn picnic table bit into Tolliver's bare ass and back as he fought his way back into consciousness. The first thing he noticed was the burning pain engulfing his face. His mouth, in particular. He ran his tongue over his teeth. Sharp pain lanced through his mouth every time he touched the exposed nerves of jagged and broken teeth—and there were certainly plenty of those. He could barely breathe through his nose, and all he could smell was blood.

"Sons of bitches broke my nose!" he shouted, voice comically nasal. He opened his eyes. He'd find those goddamn pork-chop-eating white boys and give them a taste of the ass-whooping he'd given Noriega's goons back in '89. And if they'd hurt Thompson, he'd really fuck them up.

He tried to get up and found he couldn't. Thick, scratchy ropes bound his wrists and ankles, spreading him out across the tabletop like ribs on a barbecue grill. The rough wood nipped at his flesh like a scattering of sharp teeth.

He looked up. There were so many stars, far more than he saw from downtown. The full moon looked down on him, watching him like the side-eye he got from most folk. "What are you looking at?" he shouted. "What the *fuck?*" He looked around. Scaly pine trees clustered thick around a clearing lit by what must be electric lanterns. The silent silhouettes of a crowd stood in the shadows beyond the circle of light.

"What the fuck are you looking at!" he shouted at them. "You just going to goddamn stand there? Help me!"

The crowd ignored him, as if he hadn't been speaking at all.

The wind crept over his bare skin like a cold knife scraping flesh. A shiver passed through him. He tried again to pull free of the ropes. The uneven surface clawed at his back and buttocks as he struggled.

"Don't bother," said a voice behind him. Tolliver bent his neck back over the edge of the table. A man he didn't recognize stood there in gray robes marked with what looked like blood-red Indian pictograms, watching him with cold gray eyes. "That table has held bigger, stronger men than you. *Many* bigger, stronger men."

"He ain't a man," someone snarled amid the crowd beyond the light to Tolliver's left. "He's a nigger. A fucking drunk nigger!"

Before Tolliver could snarl a reply, the robed man raised his hands. That shut up the no-good cracker in the crowd. "You see that tattoo there, on his arm? Third Marine Division. I've got the same one. It's a pity a fellow devil dog has let himself sink this low, but the least we can do is to offer him up without calling him names."

"Offer me up? What?" Tolliver demanded. "You a bunch of devil-worshippers out here?"

The robed man ignored him. "Brother Jeffrey," he called out. "Ring the bell. Call Him to us."

Tolliver connected the racist asshole's voice and the name. Jeffrey Reed, who worked at the gas station on the corner, the only white man he'd seen running a gas station in town for the last two years. The motherfucker always gave him dirty looks when he came to buy booze, but never turned down his money.

"Reed! You ungrateful Hoosier fuck!" Tolliver shouted. "I kept your goddamn gas station in business all these years! Don't think I don't know that you don't actually make any money on gas!"

Reed emerged from the crowd, rage written on blunt

features beneath a shock of dark hair. Pine straw crunched underneath the motorcycle boots the damn cracker always wore.

"Stop!" the robed man ordered. "It is the appointed hour. We can't keep Him waiting."

Reed spat. "All right," he muttered. "He'll be getting his soon enough."

"Brother Jeffrey, stop wasting time and *ring that goddamn bell.*"

Reed's boots crunched again. Then a bell tolled once, twice, three times. It sounded just like church bells, but Tolliver knew nothing remotely holy was going on here.

"You better untie me!" he demanded. "Folk'll hear that bell!"

Reed snorted. "And they'll call the Sheriff's Office, who'll tell them they'll look into it and leave us alone. Nobody's coming to save your black ass." He spat on the ground. "Goddamn worthless drunk."

The bell rang a fourth time. Tolliver looked down the length of his naked body toward where the lantern light shimmered on the surface of a dark, stagnant pond. The water extended deep into where the forest was darkest, farther than he could see. The water stirred. The insect noises of the night abruptly vanished.

Tolliver's heart froze in his chest. There was something in the water. Something heading this way.

"Behold!" the robed man shouted. "Behold, He comes!"

"He comes!" the cultists lurking in the darkness beyond the lantern light shouted in reply. "He comes! He comes!"

Tolliver strained at the ropes, his eyes locked on the water lapping the edges of the pond. His efforts raised sweat on his dark skin and rubbed his wrists and ankles raw.

"The waters are deep here," the priest intoned. "Deeper

than the ignorant carpetbaggers think. There are caverns below, dark caverns. Oh, what dwells there!"

"What dwells there!" the congregation echoed. "Oh, what dwells there!"

Ripples shot across the pond's surface. The water spilled over the dark pool's rim. Blue-green lights shined in the depths, dim and distant but growing brighter and closer. The surface of the pool began to bulge.

Tolliver refused to look away. Whatever cracker swamp-god that wanted a piece of him would have to look him in the eye.

The waters burst. Something huge rose from the water, spilling out of the pool onto the surrounding mud and grass. The glowing azure light of its many eyes reflected on slick black flesh. The cultists' howling reached new heights.

"He is here!" the priest called. "He has come!"

"He has come! He has come!"

"God!" Tolliver shouted, calling on the Lord for the first time in years. "Oh, God!"

The priest laughed. "You're not the first one to say that. I wonder if he'll answer this time?"

The creature regarded Tolliver with its solid azure eyes. Too many eyes! Tolliver squeezed his eyes closed, but the unnatural light shone through. To hell with that. He opened his eyes again and glared at the unholy thing.

"Come on then!" he shouted. "Come on, you peckerwood swamp shit!"

The eyes widened, then narrowed. Tolliver had seen that expression when he'd called out his no-good stepdaddy back in South County. But this time around, it wouldn't be *him* leaving his enemy in a pool of blood and teeth in the bad part of St. Louis.

It surged forward into the torchlight like a train of wet

black flesh. Two enormous hooked claws on the ends of too-long tentacles slammed into his chest. Ribs and wood cracked like the rifles in Panama City as the huge talons punched *through* him. Tolliver screamed, the taste of hot copper filling his mouth and spilling out over his torn lips.

"He has accepted our sacrifice!" shouted the priest. The worshippers echoed his words like a morbid church choir. Tolliver tried to curse them, but more blood than words came out.

Then the tentacles snapped back. The night air whistled over him as he hurtled through the air. The last thought he had before a mouth lined with rows of sharp white teeth engulfed him was that he'd left his arms and legs behind.

CHAPTER ONE

JAMES DALY TYPED IN THE LAST FOUR DIGITS OF HIS
Social Security number into the square white console on the
unadorned blue wall of the Edington Best Buy break room. It
beeped when he hit the big "Enter" button. *Clocked in,* he
thought as he went back out into the cavernous store. *Clock out
in three hours.*

Three hours per day four days a week during the school
year going to five hours a day five days a week during the
summer. That'd be a decent bit of money going to his car fund.
That is, if he didn't have to give Dad most of it.

This is his own stupid fault. He tried to keep his anger from
showing on his freckled face. It wouldn't do for an employee to
look pissed with customers watching. He might lose his job and
get into real trouble. Best put on a big fake smile and count the
days until he could move out. Two months until he turned eighteen. Then he could move in with Eli back in Atlanta. He
couldn't afford UNC Chapel Hill anymore, but he could work
and go to Georgia State until he could. And then he'd never
come back to Edington again.

Great. And without me around to play scary big brother, Karen might get knocked up by Sling Blade. It certainly happened enough with the locals, although never to his knowledge among the other involuntary transplants he hung out with. Though who knew what might happen the longer they stayed in this dump?

Something moved out of the corner of his eye. It was Aaron Lee, the short Korean guy who was the team lead to James and four others. He'd left the shelves brimming with cell phone accessories and was heading James' way.

Oh shit! James immediately snapped to attention. He hoped his supervisor hadn't seen him scowling and potentially annoying customers. Unhappy employees could end up fired employees real quick.

"You all right?" Aaron regarded him with his narrow brown eyes. He didn't seem angry, not yet. That was good. He remembered when his old Choi Kwong Do instructor would get mad when he made a stupid mistake. That was never fun.

James nodded quickly. "Yes sir."

"Good." Aaron pointed toward the front of the store. A tall man with thinning red hair and a goatee looked lost amid the long black shelves brimming with DVDs that lay a few yards from the double doors. "I think he needs some help."

"Yes sir."

James set off briskly across the blue carpeted floor toward the movie section and tried not to kick himself. His drifting off even for just a *moment* had gotten Aaron's attention. Though his supervisor didn't *seem* mad at him, who knows what he'd be writing in some evaluation later. He didn't need to get into trouble with the manager. Based on the traffic—or lack thereof—in the movie section, she might need to cut staff sooner rather than later.

He found the man still walking up and down the aisle like he was looking for something.

"Good afternoon, sir," James said in his most sincere voice. "Can I help you with something?"

"Yes, thank you," the customer said. His accent sounded like syrup in James' ears. "I'm looking for that movie with Sasha Baron Cohen in it..." His voice trailed off. He reddened slightly and looked down at his feet.

James kept his big fake smile going. "Do you remember what the storyline was? We have several movies with him." *None of them worth a damn, but you didn't hear that from me.*

The man thought for a moment. "It's the one where he pretends to be a foreign reporter—"

"*Bruno?*"

The man made a face. "Good heavens, not *that* one. The one where he's from Kazakhstan."

James wondered why the customer didn't want *Bruno.* Was it the rampant gayness? If it was, the man was going to get quite a surprise when the naked man fight broke out. Freaking out about that sort of thing was something James preferred to leave for Baptists, but that scene was *entirely* too long.

"I believe you're thinking of *Borat,* sir." James looked down the aisle and saw some copies lined up. "Let me get that for you. Would you prefer DVD or Blu-Ray?"

"Blu-Ray." The customer smiled proudly. "Just got a new player."

A little genuineness crept into James' smile. Despite the older man's lapse in taste, he could always appreciate someone who went the extra mile to get a quality picture. "That's awesome. The newer movies look really nice when you get them on Blu-Ray."

"Yep. And not just the new movies either. I got *Casablanca* too. Lauren Bacall's a real looker and it shows, and you can just *see* the crags in Humphrey Bogart's face."

That was odd. Back when he has money to spare, he'd bought the Blu-Ray of *Ferris Bueller's Day Off*. The movie itself didn't look any different. He'd paid an extra ten bucks he *really* should have saved for the rainy day now drenching him just to see the actors' skin flaws in more detail in the DVD extras.

Still, it looked like the Blu-Ray upgrade had worked out for this customer at least. "Wow," James said, sincerely this time. "Never heard of that before."

"It was remastered one frame at a time. Everything's so much more detailed now. It's like seeing a completely different movie."

James nodded. Part of him wanted to use the excuse of making a customer happy to keep chatting, but he could see more customers filtering in behind the man. He'd need to help as many as possible, to make up for his earlier brooding.

"I'll be sure to check it out, sir." That wasn't a *total* lie, since he'd at least swing by the Redbox at the local Walmart and see if it was there. Netflix had been one of the first casualties of the family cutbacks, before Dad had started helping himself to James' paycheck.

"Thank you for your help..."

"James. James Daly." He seriously considered saying "Bond" instead. *Nope.* That'd be lame even by his low standards.

"Excellent. I'm Sam Dixon." He extended his hand and James took it, avoiding an awkward pause. They shook, Sam's hand rougher than James'. "I'm fixing to expand my movie collection, so I might be coming back soon."

That'd be nice. There weren't many people around here as interested in film as Sam seemed to be. And if he could connect to other customers like this, the less likely he'd be laid off. There were worse places in Edington to be working than the Best Buy—some "shop and rob" convenience store or that shitty diner near the little airport came to mind—and not having a job wasn't an option.

"We'd love to see you back, sir. Thank you for shopping at Best Buy."

Sam turned smartly on his heel and walked off toward the bored-looking woman a little older than James who manned the cash register. James smiled, for real this time. However much he didn't like working at Best Buy—especially when he didn't get to keep much money—it was always good to make oneself useful.

He looked down the length of the movie aisle. A blonde-haired woman with an equally blonde-haired little daughter was in the next rack over, the one with the family movies. He set off toward them with a bit more of a spring to his step than usual. *The Fantastic Mr. Fox* had only been out on DVD a few weeks. Perhaps they might be interested in that.

CHAPTER TWO

PHILLIP DAVIDSON HANDED WHITE-HAIRED RUBY JONES the tray with her order. The blood-red barbecue sauce dripped off her pulled-pork sandwich to mingle with the yellow-white macaroni and cheese heaped beside it.

"That's seven whole dollars and fifty whole cents," he said. She had been coming here for the last twenty years, *long* before the goddamn Shane's Rib Shack had opened up, and he didn't even need to tell her the price anymore. But he still did, as he always had.

"Thank you kindly," she said, handing him the money. Exact change, as she always did.

A smile crossed his broad face, a smile that actually reached his gray eyes as his beefy hands opened the register. "You're welcome."

She turned and walked across the rough wooden floor to sit with her husband of forty years. Phillip watched them eat for a moment before his gaze drifted over to a parking lot holding only a few older cars. The Shane's Rib Shack down the road had many cars, newer cars.

He frowned. He'd been as glad as the others when the folk who worked in Atlanta started moving to Edington, especially when the last mill closed and the folk who'd lived here their whole lives had less money to spend. Most of the newcomers had made their way through the trees masking his restaurant from Fayetteville Boulevard to taste and praise his food. Business had been good.

For a while, at least. Then the tide of new arrivals became a flood. The chains, the ones they'd patronized before they moved south to Edington, soon followed. The newcomers who'd visited him largely drifted away. Not only that, but they took some longtime customers with them!

Not all of them, but a lot. There were still loyal patrons like the Joneses but the younger crowd was all but gone. They went to Shane's instead, or that Ryan's place with the all-you-can-eat pricing. It was true his fare cost slightly more, but he bought local when he could and actually paid his employees. Doing that kept business in the community; the chain parasites sent their profits elsewhere.

He frowned. Even without the mill, there was still the sheet metal plant and the furniture distribution center. Edington didn't need to make itself a "bedroom community" for the Atlanta carpetbaggers infesting the city itself and starting to ooze into the county.

He shook his head and looked away from the parking lot. Bitching wouldn't bring cars into the parking lot and customers into his restaurant.

But he knew what, or more specifically, *Who* would. The congregation he oversaw gathered in the woods and offered sacrifices, particularly the human kind, to the power that had dwelled in this land since the first Indians raised the mounds. *He* had helped the good Edington folk survive the Spanish, the British, the Federal army, and the first round of carpetbaggers the Union troops had brought with them. The second round would not be a problem for Him.

He'd just begun pondering unleashing Him on Shane's when the bell at the main door that announced visitors jangled. Phillip's gaze snapped upward. It was Sam. Phillip smiled. "How're you doing?"

"Just fine." Phillip's smile drained away. He could tell from the younger man's tenseness and waffling tone that this was a lie. This wasn't like Sam. He watched as Sam looked up at the menu and ordered a pulled-pork sandwich just like Ruby had. Phillip whistled loudly for the cooks to get on it.

"Haven't seen you in awhile," Phillip began innocently. "Everything all right at the plant?"

Sam shrugged. "Orders're still down, but there's a steady flow from China of all places. It's like there's no recession over there. I thought they made enough of that their own selves, but they're buying our sheet metal too."

Phillip pursed his lips. If it wasn't the job that was bothering him, it had to be something else. Time to be direct. "You weren't out with the rest of the congregation in the woods last week." If he'd been sick—or more likely looking after Brenda—that'd be excusable. Otherwise, not so much. With so many outsiders moving into town over the last few years, maintaining OpSec was even more important than usual.

Sam looked around. "I hadn't seen Leroy Tolliver downtown in two weeks. Knowing—"

"Not so loud!" Phillip hissed. He looked around. "You want to talk about *that*, get back here."

Phillip stepped back from the counter. A moment later, Sam came in through the two-way swinging across from the bathrooms. Phillip looked over the counter toward the dining room, then pointed at the kitchen. "Back there." The noise of the dishwasher and other machines would provide adequate cover for a quiet—and hopefully brief—conversation.

The two men withdrew to a corner in the hot kitchen beside the automatic dishwasher, well away from where one of the cooks stacked the black-edged meat for Sam's sandwich. Phillip looked straight at Sam. The younger man swallowed and began to speak. "Leroy was a drunk, and a mean one at that. But he was a veteran. Like both of us."

Phillip's spine went straight, like he was on the parade ground once again. Once a Marine, always a Marine, that was the code. Sweat beaded beneath his thinning gray hair. He grit his teeth. He'd been leading the congregation since before Sam set off across the Atlantic for Desert Storm. He wasn't going to put up with any questioning from this young pup.

The doorbell rang again, grabbing Phillip's attention. It was Bill Aiken, short and muscled from work on the county road crew, along with his very blonde and very pregnant girlfriend, Sarah Payne. Phillip frowned. Although he figured she'd make a right big order at least, the two of them really ought to get married, at least before the baby was born. From the look of her, there wasn't much time. He'd have to talk to Bill's pa, for her sake.

Rather than approach the counter, the two stood a ways off and looked over the menu on the wall. That bought time, but he'd have to get this conversation over quickly. He couldn't afford to lose any more business.

"Sam, that was no different than anything we've done before. He keeps Edington safe and prosperous; we feed Him. That's the covenant. Tolliver was a danger to the community, and He took care of that."

Phillip looked back toward the teens. They still looked at the menu on the wall. If the younger man was going to speak his piece, now was the time. He did. "Phillip, he wasn't some hippie who'd let the terrorists win. He was a—"

"You've got a one-track mind, don't you?" Phillip's voice cracked like a whip. "Tolliver's a Marine, same as me, but unlike me, he let the shit we deal with break him. All that drinking made him a goddamn worm, and He put him out of his misery. Now nobody has to tolerate him pestering them for change when they go downtown. Jimmy Thompson, our brother in the faith who owns the computer shop, has seen customers flee his store when Tolliver came around in a thirsty mood. That costs him money and if business drops enough, might cost one of his employees their jobs."

Sam stepped back toward the counter. "You don't need to get all bowed up."

"I'm not bowed up. I'm laying down the law." He gave Sam a hard look. There weren't very many congregants who'd turned traitor. He'd helped kill one at the command of the previous high priest, a murder they'd pinned on the Klan decades ago. He'd rather not do that to Sam. The younger man was a veteran, after all, and kin besides.

"But—"

Phillip leaned forward so he could whisper in Sam's ear. "You're into this up to your neck, just like me. How many sacrifices you been at? How many times was it *you* who brought Him the bacon? I can name at least two."

Sam looked at him, stone-faced. "Yes sir."

Phillip smiled and clapped him on the back. "That's a good soldier." Sam turned to head for the door back out into the restaurant. "Don't forget your sandwich. It's on the house tonight." He knew how to use both the stick *and* carrot.

The teenaged couple turned away from the menu and headed toward the counter. *Good thing they took so long to order.* Secret societies were supposed to be *secret*. It'd be hard to keep something a secret when it was getting discussed at a public barbecue restaurant, even one the carpetbaggers who wouldn't know not to ask questions rarely visited.

When Phillip returned to the counter, Sam had gotten his sandwich and for whatever reason had decided to eat it in the restaurant. The couple made their orders, which Phillip immediately set the cooks on filling. While his staff went to work, Phillip kept his eyes and ears on the couple as they chattered amongst themselves. He had to make sure they hadn't heard anything they oughtn't. If they had, they'd have to be brought before Him, to join the congregation or die. In the past people generally made the intelligent choice. The congregation's purpose was to protect the town. One didn't protect the town by killing its residents *too* often.

Fortunately, nothing they'd said or the way they looked at each other made him think they knew too much. He'd get their tags when they left and have Bowie keep an eye on them. Always better to be safe than sorry. And however much he didn't cotton to hurting a baby who hadn't been born yet, part of him wondered if He would appreciate a snack and a half.

When the couple returned to their seats, Sam drifted back toward the counter. "No more of this here," Phillip said before the younger man could even open his mouth. "Loose lips sink ships."

Sam nodded. "Understood."

"Good. Now, onto happier subjects. What've you been up to lately?"

"Well, I got a Blu-Ray player the other day. I just went by the Best Buy and got a new movie for it."

Phillip smiled. Even if Best Buy had forced some of the local electronics shops and video stores out of business, it at least provided more goods at lower prices and hired local kids besides. Some money staying in the community was better than none. And, he had to admit, they had a lot more to buy. "What movie?"

Sam frowned. "It's got Sasha Baron Cohen in it. I couldn't remember the title and one of the kids at the store helped me find it, but now I've forgotten it again."

"Hope it wasn't *Bruno*." Phillip scowled. "Queer filth, that was. I read online someone was trying to get theaters from screening that piece of crap." Luckily the local movie theater was *still* local and the owner knew just Who would be the last thing he saw if he screened that pornography. No need for a futile fight with the dissolute courts to keep everything shipshape.

"Oh no," Sam interrupted. "Not that one. The other one. *Borat*."

That one wasn't much better, with that mustachioed degenerate shoving his ass into another man's face, but Phillip had to admit he found the scene with the bear and the ice cream truck funny. "Good. That one's good for a few laughs. You and Brenda going to watch that tonight?"

Sam nodded. "Yep. Hopefully it'll lift her spirits."

Phillip nodded. Brenda was his cousin's stepdaughter. She hadn't been right since she miscarried three months ago. He reckoned she and Sam should try again in the little time they had left, but he'd read in the *Reader's Digest* that trying too soon wasn't safe. In any event, he couldn't imagine anybody getting amorous by watching that movie.

"I hope so too."

CHAPTER THREE

James turned his rattletrap blue 1998 Saab—Dad had sold his old 2004 Civic and replaced it with this piece of garbage, pocketing the difference—into Turner Glen. He deftly avoided a pothole as he descended deeper into the neighborhood in *Deliverance* country where Mom and Dad just had to move the summer before his senior year of high school. Turner Glen was a single street ending in a cul-de-sac. Five houses, only two occupied, butted up against acres of trees. Dad had to drive the whole length of the neighborhood a few times a day to make the place look busier and hopefully deter metal thieves or hobos from getting into the empty homes.

The house Mom and Dad had dragged him and Karen sixty miles into the middle of nowhere for was red brick, but leaned toward salmon-colored rather than the dark red common in downtown Edington. Black shutters flanked the windows, and there were a *lot* of windows. It was twice as big as the house they'd on Channing Drive in Buckhead.

Dad thought that big promotion meant he needed to have a house to match it. His car rumbled over some ugly cracks in the asphalt, but that didn't jolt him out of his brooding. *And the 'best value' was down here. Then the economy tanked and they let him go six months in.*

He rolled up the driveway, coming to a stop just in front of the tall wooden fence, and turned off the Atlanta classic rock station. He checked his watch. 6:45 p.m. Even though the used bookstore downtown near the courthouse kept her busy, Mom always wanted them to eat dinner together. At least the economy hadn't cost his family that comfort.

The smell of ground beef browning on the gas stove filled his nose as he walked into the kitchen from the garage. They must be having spaghetti. Saliva began gathering around his tongue. It had been awhile.

"Hey honey," Mom said, stepping away from the stove. She hugged him, her brown hair tickling him his nose. "How was work today?"

James shrugged. "Fine." He looked at the doorway between the kitchen and the family room, where Dad usually had his laptop set up. "Dad home?"

She nodded, her bright blue eyes worried. "He got in a few minutes ago. He had that interview in Atlanta today and got caught in traffic coming back."

Atlanta traffic. That was one of the few improvements moving to Edington had brought. Fayetteville Boulevard and even Fairmont Street could get crowded sometimes, but it was nothing like 400.

"Did he say how it went?"

She shook her head. "I imagine we'll be hearing that at dinner." She stepped away and returned to the stove. "Could you get the glasses out? I need to drain this and put the tomato sauce in."

"Sure."

James set the glasses out on the table, then laid out the

napkins and silverware. He was deciding whether to get out the plates as well when a radio suddenly blared in the driveway. A car door slammed shut, cutting the music off abruptly.

"Hey Karen," he said as his younger sister breezed in. She had her long hair—blonde, unlike his light brown—tied in a ponytail this time rather than wearing it loose. She set her own backpack down on the gray marble—or at least a convincing imitation thereof—counter nearest the door.

"Hey," she said as she breezed past.

"You were almost late for dinner," Mom chided. "What kept you?"

"Oh, I was just studying with Abby and a couple of her friends down at the Coffee Roasters." Shockingly enough, Edington didn't have a Starbucks, but she'd found the next best thing, as well as replacements for the musician and theatre friends she'd left behind. Pity Edington High—unlike North Atlanta High School—wouldn't be able to send her to Broadway to see how professional theater actually worked.

"Studying, eh?" James interjected. "Studying that Billy fellow, I imagine."

Karen rolled her brown eyes. "Yeah right. He has a girl-friend anyway. I'm not sure what he sees in her, but—"

James tuned out the sophomore gossip. He stepped around his sister to get the plates out of the white cabinets. He laid them out on the pseudo-granite counter beside the sink before going up the back stairs to his room. He dropped his backpack with the textbooks from his last two classes on the hardwood floor and flopped down on the bed. His feet had been hurting from standing up all afternoon and the drive home had only been a temporary respite.

He brought up his Gmail on his black smartphone. No news from those scholarships he'd applied for in the hope that he could cover books and student fees and put away money to transfer to UNC. *Damn it.* He'd gotten into Georgia State and he could pay his way through thanks to HOPE and the money from Best Buy he got to keep, but he wasn't going to let something like Dad losing his job get in the way of his dreams.

He flopped back onto his pillows. Georgia State wasn't a bad school. The area surrounding the school was a little too ghetto for his taste, but it wasn't like he didn't know how to handle himself in the city. But Chapel Hill was so much *better* than the area around Five Points. It was the best college town in the country. *Everybody* there would be his own age, and there'd definitely be lots of hot girls.

It wasn't long until Mom called the family down to dinner. Dad had emerged from the living room, the remnants of a gloomy expression clinging to his thin face, and sat at his customary position at the head of the table. Everyone sat down and, after a perfunctory blessing, set to eating.

Dad was the first to speak. "So James," he said, putting his fork down on the fabric placemat in a way that would no doubt aggravate Mom. "How was work today?"

"Just fine. Heard you had a job interview."

Dad nodded, brown eyes dropping to his plate. Not good. "It's a big firm. A lot of lawyers, mostly younger ones they work hard. Not quite where I envisioned myself working at this point in my career, but they help out a lot of local governments."

"Hopefully you'll get this," Mom said. "Government work's your bread and butter."

Dad smiled. "Thanks, hon. I wrote them a thank-you note as soon as I got back. There's another firm in Atlanta I'm looking at—"

"Any openings farther south?" James asked. "Fayetteville? Or maybe Peachtree City? All those Delta people need lawyers too." Even if Dad didn't get a job closer to Edington, at least he wouldn't spend so much driving to Atlanta. Some of that gas money would go to paying the mortgage, leaving more of James' paycheck for his college fund.

Dad sighed. "James, we've been through this. There's no future in small-town practice. Atlanta is where it is." He resumed eating, ending his part of the conversation.

Maybe no future, but it'll at least be steadier work than the freelance stuff you're doing now. James frowned. He returned to his own spaghetti. This wouldn't be the last time the issue came up.

Karen took that was an opportunity to jump in. "You *know*," she said. "It was Amber who dropped me off at the house today. She asked how you were doing."

James groaned. Amber Webb was part of the local artsy crowd his sister hung out with, although he didn't think they were close. Amber was tall and had dirty blonde hair that hung to her collarbone and eyes a mixture of gray and blue he'd never seen before. And her accent was less syrupy than he expected. James had AP Government with her last semester, and his dear sister had been doing her best to hook them up ever since.

"And *what* did you tell her?"

"Well, I mentioned you'd gotten accepted into the University of Chapel Hill as well as Georgia State. She's going to Valdosta..."

It wasn't like Amber wasn't pretty or wasn't smart. She was one of the locals who took AP classes, after all. But there was Chapel Hill, and Georgia State before that. Plenty of more suitable people there. Valdosta was so far away anyway.

"She's going to be in *Once Upon A Mattress* this summer too," Karen continued. "She's playing Princess Winifred the Woebegone. I've seen her rehearsing. She's so lively..."

James would admit to that. Amber certainly wasn't boring to hang around. But there'd be lively girls at Chapel Hill and

Georgia State. "And you're Lady Larken, right?" James interrupted.

"Of course. Thought you knew."

James really wasn't interested in community theater, or theater in general for that matter. Film allowed one to do so *much* one couldn't do on a stage. He doubted one could do *Braveheart* as a play, not if one wanted to do it justice. It'd come off looking like Monty Python, complete with coconuts.

"How're Maad and Katie doing?" Mom asked.

"Just fine so far. I don't think anybody's bothering them." Maad – Maadhav Kar – and Katie Wallace had moved down to Edington a year or two before his family did. Local tongues had started wagging when they'd gone to junior prom together and kept going when it was clear they were actually *dating*. Nothing worse than gossip had happened so far, but knowing some of the locals, Mom was right to worry.

"That's good to know."

James opened his mouth to tell them about Maad and Katie both being accepted to Georgia Tech, but something moved in the corner of his eye. James looked out the big picture window behind where his sister sat across from him. The trees pressed against the well-manicured backyard that Dad now had plenty of time to maintain, threatening to push over the sharply-honed edges of the rectangular acre of grass. Something moved in the trees, a brief flash of darker green against the brighter green of late spring.

"What's that?"

Both Mom and Dad looked out the window. Only Karen ignored him, picking at her spaghetti and idly toying with her hair.

"What's what?" Dad asked.

"I could swear I saw something move out there."

"Must be a deer," Mom said. "Lot of woods in this county. Just the other day, I saw a couple deer."

There weren't any green deer that James knew of. James didn't know where the property line was, but he'd bet it was some of the local rednecks using the woods as their personal hunting ground. While his parents returned to their dinner, he watched the trees pressing up against his family's yard for a long moment before turning away.

————

AMBER CAME to the intersection with Fayetteville Boulevard just in time to hit the last of the Atlanta commuters making their way home. Luckily the light was in her favor and the cars hadn't *completely* blocked the intersection. She swerved around a car much newer and nicer than hers jutting out into the intersection to get into the farthest of the three southbound lanes. She'd need to get over in order to eventually turn left onto Fairmont Street and head home, but that was over a mile away.

As the traffic inched its way toward the main drag and some annoying pop song prattled on the radio, Amber had time to think. And think.

James. James with his wit that was actually *funny* instead of just lame and brains that didn't come with being a know-it-all, unlike annoying Walter. James with his bright blue eyes and freckles. His many, many freckles. She'd driven his sister home that night, but she never saw *him*. His car was in the driveway, so he *had* to be home. But he didn't come out to say hello.

She snorted. Maybe he actually had something important to do, like study for the last finals. Or something with college. Perhaps he was getting a start ordering the things he needed online, where he could find more at lower prices than anywhere Edington could offer. Someone like him would have things going on, things more important than *her*.

Face it. He's just not into you.

She still wondered *why*. From what Karen told her he'd never dated anybody in Edington. He'd even *skipped senior prom*. The only thing Karen ever said about his personal life in Atlanta was a girl he'd dated briefly a year before. He wasn't like some of the boys in Edington who just wanted one thing and then dropped girls like hot potatoes when they'd had their fun.

Could he be gay? She shook her head. Although those so inclined in Edington weren't too obvious about it if they knew what was good for them, she could tell. And James gave off none of the signals.

Maybe he thought himself too good for girls from Edington. Girls like her. Someone from Buckhead probably reckoned Edington folk were all dumb hicks. She tried to resent him for that. But it didn't last. He didn't seem mean either. Of course, he wouldn't openly disdain his classmates, not if he were smart. But she could tell if someone was phony. She wasn't a stupid sophomore anymore.

Or maybe it was her cheekbones. She looked at herself in the rear-view mirror. Did they stick out too much? Or was it her nose? It was always a little bit wide. She shook her head. James couldn't possibly be that shallow. It couldn't be that.

The thought of asking Karen more about what made him tick rose into her mind. Her fair skin reddened slightly, even though nobody else was in the car to see her. Was she really thinking to conspire with his *sister*? Well, more than what she was doing already...

She shook her head. *Girl, you're overthinking it. Just be cool.*

Guys didn't like girls who were *too* eager. She didn't want him to think she was like that crazy woman from *Vanilla Sky*. And she had more important things to think about anyway. The first rehearsals for *Once Upon A Mattress* were coming up soon. She had the lead female part, so she had to know her lines and know them *well*. Her little sister Claire should be home from soccer practice by the time she finally got through the traffic and back home. Claire could help her rehearse.

She turned her attention back to the traffic. During her brooding, she'd passed by the big Ford dealership and was now inching past the whitewashed Sears shopping plaza and the Wendy's where she used to work. It wouldn't be long until she could turn out of the sea of cars onto Fairmont and be on her way.

She smiled. Her brooding was good for taking her mind off the traffic at, least.

CHAPTER FOUR

FRIDAY CAME, AND WITH IT THE BEST BUY SCHEDULE FOR the coming week. For the first time in nearly a month, James had a weekend totally free! And since the mortgage payment wasn't due until the end of the month, he got to keep most of that week's paycheck.

That called for a celebration. After he had finished that afternoon's shift, James texted Maad and Katie. He'd have liked to call Eli too, but he wouldn't like making the drive to Edington, especially on such short notice. Fortunately Maad's friend Alex Bello was also up for dinner, so James wouldn't be a third wheel.

James got to the Zaxby's north of downtown first. Next came Maad, tall and dark-skinned with a goatee. Alex, lanky and sporting a goatee as well, came on his heels. Last was Katie, shorter than Maad and with easily-sunburned skin and red hair. They clustered in a booth by the door, one of the few unoccupied by families. Maad got chicken fingers that James bet his vegetarian parents wouldn't like him eating, while James ordered a sandwich with fries.

As James ate, he studied the memorabilia lining the wall above the booth so typical of a Zaxby's. A golden sign advertising whale-watching in Santa Barbara caught his attention. "That looks interesting." He pointed. "I'd like to see it, if I ever get the chance to head out there."

"I've done it," Alex said around a mouthful of the spicy crinkle fries. "It's awesome. You go out in this little boat and then the whales come. They're so much bigger than you, but they're alive, not airplanes or ships. I was thirteen when I went out, but I can still remember it. Clear as a photo."

That made James want to do it even more. Maybe he should start assembling a "bucket list." After he graduated from UNC Chapel Hill with that business degree, of course. He'd need a good job to afford to vacation in California.

The restaurant door banged open. Katie jerked her head up. "Boys," she warned. "Heads up."

A trio of locals had just arrived. The tallest was brown-haired Tommy McCabe, who James had the misfortune of sharing his honors calculus class with. On his heels came Bill Aiken, who'd been in James' health class before he dropped out. Trailing *him* was blonde and bitchy—and pregnant—Sarah Payne.

Great, James thought. *I hope they don't want to sit anywhere near us.* He looked around. Unfortunately there was an open booth that'd accommodate four or five people right next to them, and none of the smaller tables he could see were available.

"Hey Maad," Alex said. "Maybe you and Katie could sit there? James and I, we wouldn't want to be a third and a fourth wheel interfering with—"

As if Alex couldn't be more obvious. James shook his head. "Let's just finish up and get out of here."

They didn't finish up quickly enough. The locals got their

orders and filled up the big booth. Sarah's disapproving expression fell on Maad and Katie, as it often did, before it shifted to James. It wasn't long before the rest of her friends got involved.

"Hey!" Tommy said. "Y'all talking about us?"

"No," Alex immediately replied. That would mollify them, hopefully. Then he and his friends could get back to their dinner in peace.

Tommy snorted. "Bullshit." He looked from James to Alex. "It might've been that one, or might have been you." He smiled, teeth crooked in his narrow mouth. "Can't tell. You Atlanta folk all sound alike."

"They think they're better than us," Bill cut in. He pointed an accusing finger at James. Sarah glared at him, but Bill kept on talking. "That one's dad's a big-shot lawyer in Atlanta. Except he lost his job. Didn't he, you carpetbagger?"

Carpetbagger? *Carpetbagger?* Was he serious? He couldn't be more of an asshole redneck if he *tried*. James rolled his eyes. Then the *perfect* retort sprang into his mind. "Well at least I didn't knock up my girlfriend and have to drop out of school."

That certainly struck home. Bill jumped up from his seat. James rose to his feet. Anger raced through him like a forest fire, but an undercurrent of icy fear nipped at its heels. Working on the county road crew had made Bill bigger and stronger. He could take a lot of hits before he went down, but he'd only need one or two before he knocked James on his ass. Then he'd get a taste of those big leather boots Bill wore.

He didn't want to get his ass kicked, but he'd show the stupid redneck that he wouldn't be pushed around. It'd been a long time since he'd taken Choi Kwong Do, but it didn't require a lot of skill to kick another man in the nuts.

Alex jumped up beside James. Tommy's arm snapped out and grabbed Bill by the arm. Bill jerked back, stopped before he could step away from the booth. "You dumbass," Tommy snapped. His voice fell to a harsh whisper James could barely hear. "Your dad works at the plant this punk's dad runs." He pointed at Alex. "The old man won't like his son getting his ass kicked. You want your dad to lose his job? You won't be able to support Sarah and the rest of your folks just working on the road crew."

"Yeah," Sarah hissed. "Don't be a fucking fool."

James's gaze wandered over to Alex, who smiled smugly. His father managed the Caterpillar plant in the next town where a lot of locals worked. James bet he'd brag about how he'd saved James from getting a beat-down from some hick for quite a while.

Maad sighed in relief. James knew his parents. He'd have gotten in trouble for any fight regardless of who started it. They probably thought Georgia Tech would rescind his acceptance if the cops were ever called on him, even if the charges didn't stick.

"You think we should just sit here and take their shit?" Bill demanded. "This is *our* town, not theirs. When gas goes back up again, they'll all move out, but we'll still be here."

Tommy smiled. "I've got a better idea." He turned and looked James straight in the eye. James' breath caught in his throat, but he didn't lower his eyes. "I bet you Atlanta folk think you can do anything better than we can. Care to prove it?"

"Sure," Alex said. James suppressed the urge to groan. What sort of pissing contest was the idiot going to get them into?

"Well then," Tommy said. "There's a big patch of cleared land down on Newnan Road, past Johnson Drive. They were going to make it one of those new neighborhoods, but when the recession came the money fell through. They did cut a long-ass road through it."

Bill tensed. "That's down by the tree farm, isn't it?" He looked at Tommy. "What do you want to do down there?"

James narrowed his eyes. Something about that property had the belligerent asshole all spooked. Maybe that was where some of the older dropouts cooked meth. This *was* a small town, after all.

"Bill and I both have ATVs," Tommy continued. "Us three and a friend of mine will race the four of you. Tomorrow, four o'clock."

"It's on," Alex said triumphantly. "You're not on the only one with an ATV." Alex looked over at Maad and Katie. James' eyes widened slightly. Did Alex think they'd really go along with this?

"The tree farm would be private land, would it not?" Maad asked. He did not look enthusiastic in the slightest. "You want to get us all arrested for trespassing?"

Tommy snorted. "There's plenty of empty land between that neighborhood and the tree farm. Besides, even if we *do* get into the tree farm, who's gonna know we were there? It's not like it's guarded." He looked straight at Maad, ignoring Bill's uneasy expression. "Come on. They won't kick you out of Georgia Tech over something like this."

Maad swallowed. "All right." After a moment, Katie nodded.

Then everyone's gazes fell on James.

James tensed. He really didn't want to get into another pissing contest with the locals, especially not Saturday when he'd planned to see if Eli wanted to play paintball. Less than a hundred days until he could walk away from this shithole. He'd be meeting these yahoos on their own ground, away from any friendly witnesses. Dad would think this a really stupid idea and for the first time since he'd dragged the family to Edington, he'd be right about something.

On the other hand, he'd be damned if he looked like a pussy in front of these morons and his own friends. Even Alex. For a moment he was tempted to claim he had to work. Let Alex deal with the situation his big mouth had gotten them all into.

Then he looked at Maad and Katie. They were going along with this idiocy, however reluctantly. They'd go with Alex toward what Dad called a "pipe farm" and the tree farm beyond that, for a dangerous race or—quite possibly—a beat-down from a bunch of belligerent rednecks.

James scowled. He wasn't going to puss out on Maad and Katie at least. And if all four of them showed up, maybe Tommy and Bill would think better about picking a fight. His gaze crept over to Bill. He'd need to keep an eye on that redneck especially.

James tried to keep the irritation out of his voice. "Tomorrow's not going to be your lucky day. I'm in."

Tommy grinned, crooked teeth white in his hatchet face. "Good to know you can come. Y'all best be practicing."

"Oh we will," Alex said.

James resisted the urge to groan.

CHAPTER FIVE

The bright afternoon sun lit up the blue sky as James set off for the ATV race. Mom was at the bookstore and Dad was off on errands somewhere, so he'd left a note saying where he'd be. He could have called or texted, but better to ask forgiveness than permission. And he'd be eighteen soon anyway—it wasn't like he needed to worry about "stranger danger" just leaving the house.

Getting to the "pipe farm" was easy at first. Newnan Road was a four-lane straight shot east out of town, past where Maad's folks lived and where Karen said Amber lived. There was one turn, drive another couple miles, and turn again.

The second turn took James down a long two-lane road. No strip malls here, or even gas stations. Only a few shabby old houses that got fewer and farther between as he drove deeper into the woods. The towering trees pressed against the road from both sides, their roots sometimes pushing through gaps in the concrete curbs. Their canopies arched overhead, blocking out the sun for long stretches. At one point, James passed over an iron bridge soaked with bloody rust spanning a slow, dark creek.

Son of a bitch. I can already hear the banjos.

For a moment he thought about turning back. It wouldn't be hard to say he had to cover for someone else at Best Buy at the last minute. It's not like Tommy and Bill would actually check. Hell, he could say his parents learned what he was doing and grounded him. That's what they always told him to say if someone tried to get him to do something stupid, like smoke weed.

He snorted. He wasn't going to get shown up by some stupid rednecks. Disappearing would give them just the opening to rag his ass until the day he left. And then they'd take credit for him leaving. And there was no way he was going leave Maad and Katie alone with them. And Alex too, even though the whole situation *was* that idiot's fault.

He'd check to make sure Maad and Katie were actually *there*, of course. He picked up his phone. He'd call Maad. Maybe he'd decided to skip out and take Katie with him. Knowing some of these people that'd be a really good idea.

Only one bar. Shit. Out here in the sticks, his signal would be crap. He gave it a try anyway. The call went straight to voicemail. *Well shit.* Maad's parents made him put away even more money for college than James had to pay Dad, so it wasn't like he had a top of the line phone to start with.

Up ahead, just past an old wooden shotgun house whose collapsed roof teemed with ivy and even a tiny pine tree, the road turned to gravel. James swallowed. Yep. *Deliverance* country for sure. He turned on the radio and switched it to his favorite classic-rock station. A little bit of Guns and Roses would lighten the mood. He frowned. It just *had* to be "Welcome to the Jungle," didn't it?

After a hundred yards, the road turned back into asphalt.

The forest stopped abruptly after another dozen yards. The sudden brightness after so long in the gloom stabbed at James' eyes. He squinted, slowing down in case something got in his way.

The road ahead snaked into a mostly-cleared area. White plastic pipes rose from amid tall green grass and even spindly young pines. That must be why the "pipe farm" got its name. But where were the others? The unwanted image of Maad hanging from a tree rose into his mind.

He found the others soon enough, at a cul-de-sac mere yards from where the far end of the aborted subdivision opened onto a larger road cutting through another set of woods.

Why the hell didn't they tell me to go in that end? I could've avoided this whole adventure entirely.

It had to be a trick. They probably had him go in that way to mess with his head. *Clever.* It had to have been Tommy's idea; James doubted Bill much appreciated "book learning." Redneck psychological warfare.

Alex, Maad, and Katie were already there, nearly clinging to Alex's shiny green Cadillac in the middle of the cracked asphalt. And unfortunately, so were Tommy, Bill, Sarah, and some black kid James didn't know. *They* stood near a gigantic— if somewhat dented in places—pickup truck. Behind it lay an equally large trailer bearing two banged-up ATVs. All four locals wore camo. James cocked his head. Given how these losers acted toward Maad and Katie, he'd figured they had a bunch of white robes in their closets.

Of course, everybody says *one of their best friends is black.*

Maad's gaze fell on James as he drove up. The relief on his dark face was obvious. He must've been waiting for a beat-down the whole time.

James pulled his car between his friends and the locals. Tommy approached as he climbed out. "Took you long enough." He spat on the wet ground. "I was wondering if maybe you'd pussed out after all." That drew a glare from Sarah, which Tommy ignored. "Wouldn't want to disappoint Bill here."

"I wouldn't either." James was getting sick and tired of the chips these losers were carrying around on their shoulders. He'd teach that jackass a lesson in manners. "So where're we going to race?"

"Y'all follow me," Tommy ordered. He pointed to a gap in the thick pine trees just beyond the pickup truck. James followed, with Alex, Maad, and Katie trailing behind. It was more than a little bit warm in his blue Tarheels sweatshirt, but he resisted the urge to take it off. Once they got rolling, it would get chilly real quick.

"All right," Tommy said. "You and Bill are going first. He"— he pointed to Alex—"and I will race next. Sarah's not in any condition to participate, but she's raced this way before and I can compare Katie here's time against hers. Last'll be Gracen and..." His voice trailed off. He looked at Maad "What *was* your name again?"

"Maad." The Indian's response was like the crack of a gunshot, but James doubted Tommy knew or cared just how irritated Maad was. Tommy just nodded.

Of course *you'd pair off the only non-whites. Don't want to lose to Kumar, do you?*

Bill hopped onto the black metal trailer and then the ATV. James climbed up behind him. He had barely gotten onto his ATV and put on the helmet hanging from the handlebars when Bill's engine roared loud beside him.

James looked down at the pebbled handlebars. It had been a long time since he'd ridden an ATV.

"All right," Bill said. "Can you turn it on, or do you need me to do it?" James ground his teeth at the insult in the redneck's voice. He could do it himself, thank you very much.

"Hold on." There was a big red button on the right handle-bar. That looked like it'd start the damn thing. He pressed the button. Nothing happened.

Shit! He pressed the button harder. Maybe this was one of things one had to press the button a bunch of times fast, or maybe hold it down. Maybe it was like Dad's goddamn leaf blower and its choke—

Bill snorted. "Okay, quit that. You'll mess it up." James sighed. He hated to admit it, but Bill probably was better with the ATV. "You've got to turn the brake on. It's a safety feature." Bill smiled coldly. "Wouldn't want you to go flying off and end this race before I beat you." Bill peered at James' handlebars. "It's already in neutral, and the engine kill switch is off. That's good. The choke's engaged."

"Okay."

Bill sighed, leaned over and clicked some things on the handlebars. The rear brake lights flared red. "Now press the button." James pressed the button. The engine roared to life. "Now disengage the choke!" Bill shouted over the thundering engine. "It'll stall!" James looked at the handlebars. Lawn-mowers had chokes, but he didn't see anything like one. He could feel his cheeks turning red. He'd lose the race before he'd even started. Everyone would laugh at him...

Bill sighed. "Pull the damn lever right!"

James did so. The engine rumbled like it should. He sighed in relief, hoping Bill didn't see him. The local gave no sign, instead slowly rolling off the trailer toward the woods. After a moment, James followed, keeping the acceleration to a mini-mum. He didn't want to make the kind of mistake that could put him in the hospital, or for that matter, the morgue.

Bill circled the cul-de-sac, with James trailing behind. The others followed on foot, Tommy and Alex watching the most eagerly of all. Maad and Katie—and surprisingly, Gracen—still hung back. Bill led them toward a lot where the grass and baby trees were thinnest. Ahead lay a gravel path that the dark woods soon swallowed whole.

"Okay everybody," Tommy shouted over the growling engines. "Bill's more familiar with the terrain hereabouts, so he'll describe the route."

Bill cleared his throat. "All right." A moment passed. Then he started speaking quickly. "Go straight ahead as the crow flies until you hit the fence. That's the edge of the tree farm. We're *not* trespassing there. Go right and drive until you see a footbridge over the creek. Cross it. Go until you find the hunting blind. Some of the folk who hunt here don't pick up after themselves. Find something they left and bring it here. First one wins."

Something was definitely eating at him. A quick glance showed that Gracen kept looking at the woods, then looking away. Only Tommy and Alex seemed to be enjoying themselves. James shrugged. If Bill were afraid of something, that'd benefit him. Even though he hadn't been on an ATV in years, he at least wasn't afraid. A small smile cracked his face. He might have a chance of beating the redneck after all.

"Pretty simple, right?" Tommy said. "Couldn't take more than half an hour tops. Both ATVs are gassed up."

"No more than half an hour," Bill repeated. James looked over at him. As soon as their eyes met, a cocky grin replaced the uneasiness ruling Bill's face. "Best leave the engine running when you stop to pick up their trash. I don't want to have to turn it on for you *again*."

James pondered the route. "That doesn't seem far at all."

Bill's good humor immediately vanished. "It doesn't look that way as the crow flies. But on foot or even on an ATV..." His voice trailed away. He looked around. "The quicker we get this done, the better."

"You—" James bit off "scared." He didn't want to pick a fight out here, far from friendly ground, with somebody twice his size.

Bill's head snapped up. "Am I what?"

"Sure it's that far?" James finished. Relief washed through him. A quick and witty response was usually better than a fight.

Bill sighed. "Just take my word for it, okay? Just because you're going to graduate doesn't mean you know everything."

The words touched something deep inside James. Although Bill's situation was his own damn fault, he still wasn't living up to his full potential. And he'd be a father soon. A kid shouldn't suffer because of his parents' bad judgment. That wasn't fair, not fair at all.

"You know," James said. "I'm sure there're places around here you can study for a GED—"

"We can discuss this later." Bill's face brooked no argument. "Right now, let's race."

"All right!" Tommy called. "You both ready?" Bill nodded. After a second, so did James. "Then on your mark, get set." He grinned theatrically. "Aaaannnd GO!"

The whirling wheels spat gravel as Bill rocketed off. James pushed the accelerator button on the handlebar down about halfway and set off after him. He kept a light touch on the button. Best not accelerate too fast and flip the damn thing.

Bill surged over the cracked curb. His wheels crushed grass and a pine sapling no taller than an end table when he landed. James followed. When the ATV slammed into the ground, the seat slammed into James' crotch. His eyes bulged. He wondered if Bill were wearing a cup or something. It would be an awfully inglorious race if he couldn't drive fast for fear of crushing his nuts.

James pushed the button harder. The engine roared. The ATV bounced harder across the uneven ground. He tightened his grip on the handlebars and continued accelerating. He hadn't wanted to get into this, but he'd be damned if he were going to lose.

Seconds later, they passed under the trees. Though plenty of light filtered through the trees at first, it wasn't long before the branches overhead grew thick and wild. Gloom devoured the once-sunny woods. The air whipping across James' exposed face and hands cooled. The ground dipped. Bill's ATV vanished from sight before emerging once more like those whales Alex had talked about at Zaxby's. James swore and sped up. Just a little. He didn't want to go flying. He crashed through fallen limbs, hard on the tracks Bill's ATV had cut into the wet ground.

It wasn't long before a gray chain link fence rose ahead. Coils of razor wire rolled along the top.

A lot of security for a tree farm. He rolled his eyes. *They afraid someone'll come in and get a free Christmas tree?*

James turned the handlebars right and rode alongside the fence, following where treads marred the slurry of wet earth and leaves. The river of interlocking metal rolled to James' left for quite a while. *Must be a damn big tree farm.* Maybe it was secretly a pot farm. He'd heard about the gangs growing weed in some of the big parks out West.

Then a wide dark pool bisected by the fence opened up in front of him.

"Holy shit!" He tore the handlebars as far to the right as he could. The ATV's two left wheels left the ground. The right wheels tore into mud. Cool, heavy wetness spattered his legs. James' mouth worked silently, hands gripping the handlebars so tightly his knuckles hurt. The ATV's left wheels slammed down into the dark water, soaking his already muddy legs to the hip and giving his left side a good spraying. Water rooster-tailed from the tires. Soon all four tires caught solid ground, and he was on his way again.

His heartbeat slowed just a little as he rolled alongside the pond. The dark waters extended pretty far away from the fence before narrowing into a murky creek. Though the mud was uncomfortable on his legs, he smiled anyway.

The bridge had to be close.

———

It hung suspended in the dark waters, so deep that light itself was only a distant flicker overhead. Its large azure eyes were closed. It typically spent most of the day like this, not truly asleep but not truly awake either. It would go deeper to truly sleep, into the dark abyssal caverns where it could trust that nothing would bother it.

Something rumbled in the distance, the sound distorted by the pillar of water overhead. Its many eyes slid open, casting a glow throughout the dim waters all around. Those noises were new to its vast domain. The red men who called themselves "Istichata" and "Muskogee" who'd once brought it food never had them. It was only the white and sometimes black men called "Americans" who did, but only recently.

It wasn't hungry. A deer had come to drink at one of the ponds scattered across its wide domain not long before. The sharp antlers had hurt when its vast mouth had engulfed the struggling prey, but its throat was wide enough the deer didn't catch as it thrashed its way down.

But not all Americans offered it food. Some preyed on the deer and other animals, eating food it could eat. These humans were trespassing. It knew how to deal with trespassers.

A flick of its vast tail sent it on its way.

JAMES RODE ALONGSIDE THE CREEK. It had been quite a while since he left the pond behind. Where was the bridge? It wasn't hard to believe Bill had given him bad directions just so he'd get lost. His eyes dropped to the gas gauge. He had plenty. He could figure his way back if it were some dirty trick.

The ground dipped suddenly in front of him. James hit the brakes too late. The ATV hung suspended in the air for a moment before dropping like a stone. It careened downward, James holding onto the handlebars for dear life.

Ohshitohshitohshit. He bounced up and down, barely holding on. Each impact slammed him crotch-first onto the seat. Pain flared with each blow. Stars danced in his reddened vision. The low ground alongside the creek was wet. The tires caught in the mud, the resulting brown rooster-tails soaking his already sopping jeans and even marring his sweatshirt.

Thankfully the ATV didn't get stuck or fall over. It continued up the hill, slowing as it advanced. Just before it would have crested the hill, it slowed to a stop.

Shit!

The ATV started to roll backward. James jammed the accelerator button all the way down. The engine roared. For one terrible second the ATV kept sliding. Then the ridged tires caught the ground, throwing brown dirt and decayed leaves. The soil-scent of rot tickled his nostrils. The ATV clambered up the hill.

The bridge lay ahead. James surged across before he had time to wonder if its moss-stained wood could take the ATV's weight. A quick glance behind showed him the bridge was still there. There were wet, fresh tracks in the mud ahead. James grinned. It wasn't over yet!

James caught up sooner than he'd thought. The first thing

he saw was dirt rising in the air, flung by the other ATV. Then even that vanished from sight as Bill pulled ahead.

James drove the ATV harder. Based on what his rival had said earlier, it couldn't be that far to the hunting blind. Bill would get there first, get some crap the slovenly locals had left, and be on his way before James could even come to a stop. And then they'd be laughing at him for *months*.

James accelerated once more. The bouncing increased. He grit his teeth. He'd beat Bill there no matter how much it hurt his balls. Hitting the wet ground faster than before threw more mud onto his legs, but he did his best to ignore it and kept his eyes peeled for the other ATV.

The ATV rolled upward. Below, where the ground descended once more, he spotted Bill. James laughed. Bill wasn't that far ahead. James continued accelerating. He'd beat that redneck yet!

His elation didn't last long. The ATV shot off the hill. Its wheels turned in empty air. When he landed, it was going to hurt like hell. James stood on the footrests as the ATV slammed into the wet ground.

Standing up might've saved his balls, but he realized too late he shouldn't have locked his knees. Pain roared up both his legs at the impact. He shouted.

Bill looked back and laughed. "Enjoying yourself?" he called, voice barely audible over the roaring engines. James reddened. He just *had* to do that in front of Bill, and Bill just *had* to notice.

Another dark pond opened up ahead, its steep walls barely confining its murk. Bill was looking back at James. He couldn't possibly see what lay ahead.

James pointed. "Look out!" He hoped his voice carried over the roar of both their engines.

Bill's gaze followed James' finger. The redneck immediately yanked the handlebars right. His left two wheels lost their grip on the dark earth. Bill threw himself to the left, but even his bulk wasn't enough to compensate. The ATV went over. James could swear he heard something crunch.

OH SHIT!

James tore his wheel to the right, circling around the toppled ATV. Bill lay screaming on the leafy wet ground, the toppled ATV pinning both his legs. James' eyes darted all over the ATV controls. How could he turn the thing off? And if he did, would he be able to turn it back on? He didn't want to rely on Bill, especially now.

He squeezed both brake handles as hard as he could. The ATV's abrupt stop slammed him forward. The pain in his knees and balls flared again. He took his hands off the brakes. The ATV stayed where it was. Luckily its engine kept running.

James hopped over to Bill. The bigger youth pushed at the ATV, but even with arms swollen by hard work on the roads he could barely get it off the ground.

"It's up," Bill gasped. "Hold it up while I—" he breathed in and moaned in pain—"get out."

James nodded quickly. "Got it." He reached down and grabbed hold of the vehicle's leather seat.

"Ready?"

James tightened his grip. "Yep."

"All right." Bill let go abruptly. The whole weight of the ATV slammed onto James' hands like a falling sledgehammer. James pushed up with all he could. It wasn't long before the exertion made him tremble.

He managed to hold the ATV off the ground long enough for Bill to swing his right leg out from under its vast metal bulk. The seat slipped from his hands before Bill could drag his left leg—spattered with blood—completely out from under the boxy metal beneath the seat. He shouted in pain as the ATV slammed back down on the side of his calf.

"Sorry," James muttered sheepishly. He could feel his face reddening. Just how much of a goddamn pussy was he that he couldn't hold up the ATV for more than a moment?

"Son of a bitch!" Bill swore. He sat up and grabbed the seat with both hands. James followed suit. Together they pushed the bulky vehicle up just enough to get Bill's leg free. Bill worked his way backward, wincing with each incremental move. Though James kept his hands on the seat, he wasn't pushing up as much as before. The seat dragged at his fingers. James' hands and arms protested. He grit his teeth. Bill's leg looked bloodier than it had before. He'd barely made Second Class when he was in the Scouts, but he knew a compound fracture broke the skin. *Shit.*

The ATV dipped, not enough to drive Bill's leg back into the mud, but enough for the metal to kiss his bloodied camouflage pants above the ankle. Bill snarled.

"Sorry about that," James said quickly.

"Goddamn it," Bill growled. "Don't fucking drop it!"

"I won't, I won't, don't worry." He pulled harder, muscles burning. The ATV slowly rose. Despite the situation, a smile crossed his broad face. If he got the ATV back onto all four wheels, then he wouldn't have to hold it up anymore.

James pushed with his knees and back. Though the seat bore down on his hands and the muscles along his spine trembled, the ATV kept rising. The weight against his fingers lessened as he strained against the bulky machine. Eventually the seat pulled away from his hands as the ATV fell back onto all four wheels.

"Good," Bill hissed through clenched teeth. "I can ride it back out."

"With the broken leg?" James protested. "Maybe it'd be better if..."

His voice trailed away. Other than the low rumble of his ATV's engine, surrounding woods were totally quiet. No birds, not even the buzzing of insects. The hairs on the back of his neck rose. He looked around. Nothing moved in the endless trees surrounding them. Bill looked around, fear soon etching itself into his harsh features. James swallowed. His hands trembled despite himself. "What's going—"

He never got the chance to finish his sentence.

The waters of the pond stirred, sloshing against the black mud holding them prisoner. James stepped back. The hairs on the back of his neck stood at full attention now. His skin crawled. He looked left and right. He and Bill were all alone amidst the trees and the vines rooted in their wooden flesh, alone with whatever was in the water.

"What the hell is that?" James' voice rose embarrassingly high. "What's down there?"

Bill's blue eyes were locked on the bestirred water. "Son of a bitch!" Bill swore. He scrambled back as best he could, dragging his broken leg behind him.

Azure lights appeared in the depths. The lights were part of something big and dark, something James couldn't quite see. The corn muffins he'd eaten for breakfast stirred uncomfortably in his stomach and the back of his mouth. Trembling raced up his legs. Sweat beaded beneath his hair and under his arms.

Okay, we're a lot farther south than Atlanta. Maybe that's just an alligator, just an alligator, just an...

Then the darkness surged upward, forcing the murky waters up over the pond's edge and over James' feet. It rose high, blocking what little sun peeked through the trees and casting both Bill and James in shadow lit only by azure lights.

Now it was James' turn to scream. Wet warmth bloomed

within his pants. He scrambled back toward his ATV, thanking the God he rarely prayed to the engine was still running. He had to get away, had to get away from the thing, that terrible thing looking over them with a mouth that was as big as a...

"Don't leave me!" Bill howled. Still dragging his broken leg behind him, he pulled himself over the wet, leaf-strewn earth after James.

His words seized James' attention. James looked back just in time for a pair of tentacles to shoot forward and slam Bill belly-first into the ground. The impact with the wet earth cut off his pained scream. Then the tentacles snapped backward, hoisting Bill into the air. White claws streaked with bright red blood glared out of Bill's chest like a pair of murderously angry eyes. Bill kept rising, like a morbid puppet on slick black strings. His pain-maddened eyes bulged in his head. His mouth worked, spilling blood like tears.

"Run, you dumb carpetbagger," he burbled.

Then the tentacles yanked him backward. Bill folded into a cavernous mouth with rows upon rows of sharp white teeth that reminded James all too much of something he'd seen on Shark Week.

James staggered backward on legs rapidly turning to jelly. He had to get back on his ATV and get the hell away before he ended up kebabbed too. He threw himself onto the vehicle, not giving a damn about his balls, and grabbed hold of the accelerator on the handlebar.

The sound of something huge wallowing in the mud thundered behind him, the sound piercing the engine's roar. He threw a glance back. It was coming his way, a like a freight train made of calamari.

Oh shit oh shit oh shit oh shit.

The blue-green orbs—they were definitely eyes—were locked on him. Blood shined on black flesh. James accelerated, uncaring if he hit something and flipped just so long as he was away from that *thing* coming out of the dark water. The ATV's engine roared. He erupted forward just as something flashed toward his face.

A blow to his left cheek nearly knocked him off the ATV. There was no pain at first, but soon agony erupted across his face. He held onto the handlebars for dear life, every bump and variation in their rubber coating digging into his hands. The vehicle carried him away from whatever the hell it was that had taken Bill. The huge black bulk faded into the distance behind him with a frustrated roar that sounded a lot like an alligator.

James turned his attention back to the path ahead. Having gotten away from some fucking tentacle monster, now he had to get back to the others and warn them to get the hell out of there before it came for them, came for them to *eat* them. Snotty Alex or bitchy Sarah shouldn't be food. Hell, not even *Tommy* deserved that.

The left shoulder of his sweatshirt suddenly felt strangely warm. He spared a glance downward.

The soft blue fabric was dark with blood.

CHAPTER SIX

TOMMY HAD TAKEN ONE LOOK AT JAMES' BLOODIED FACE and called the race off. James wasn't sure what he'd told the others, but Sarah had screamed and tried to rush off into the woods. It had taken Tommy and Gracen both to stop her. Then they'd bundled him into Tommy's truck—Katie had taken James' keys—and they'd taken him straight to the county emergency room not far from Fairmont Street. Tommy stayed with Sarah, who sat weeping in the hallway clutching her swollen belly while Maad, Katie, and Alex followed him into the cold emergency room as far as the nurses would let them. They'd shooed the trio away, then numbed his face and stitched him up.

Just when he thought they were about to let him go, a quartet of sheriff's deputies in brown uniforms showed up. Somewhere in all the hubbub, someone must've dialed 911. They led the others away, leaving James alone with the biggest deputy.

"So," the lawman said, his cool blue eyes unreadable. Dark hair fringed with gray peeked out from underneath a wood-brown baseball cap emblazoned with the logo of the Sheriff's Office. The big man drew a cigarette from his pocket. As an annoyed nurse looked on, he lit it and took a drag. "Got a phone call a few minutes ago. Bill Aiken went out for a race with you and didn't come back." He loomed over James like a mountain.

"Yeah," James said. Sweat began beading on his forehead. Years of the things he'd learned from having a lawyer for a father raced through his head. For starters, one way people got into trouble was trying to be helpful and letting things slip. He swallowed. Best guard his tongue, lest he give the rednecks some excuse to charge him with murder. He swallowed. "I don't have to talk to you without a lawyer."

The deputy scowled. "Who told you that?"

James' jaw worked. "AP U.S. Government. And my dad's a lawyer."

The deputy raised an eyebrow. "He coming?"

James nodded. Maad had called soon after they left the pipe farm. Dad had gotten home by then, but home was well north of the hospital. Even during the weekend, it'd take a while to get down Fayetteville Boulevard to the hospital.

James looked toward the examining room's wooden door. He could hear the usual hospital bustle on the other side, but no sign of Dad. His heart began racing. He looked at the nurse. Hopefully she wouldn't leave him alone while some redneck implemented the third degree. He'd heard if you put a phone book on somebody and hit them with a hammer, it'd hurt like hell but not leave a bruise.

The nurse looked at her watch and stepped through the doorway. James was left alone with the deputy. Despite emptying his bladder not long before, he suddenly needed to piss again. He didn't see any phone books lying around, but who knew what the local could think of. The deputy certainly looked like he had ample experience. Luckily she left the door partway open.

The deputy paced in front of the brown examination chair where the doctors had done their work. James nervously smoothed out the teal scrubs he wore over the fresh—thank God—underwear they'd given him while the local cops no doubt examined his clothes.

"All right," the deputy said. "We can wait a spell."

Time passed. James looked out the doorway into what little of the hallway he could see. No Dad. He didn't see any of the deputies or his friends either. At least they weren't being taken out of the hospital in handcuffs. He nearly snorted. The hospital was a big place. If the locals decided to make them disappear, they could just lead them out of the back of the building. Fewer witnesses that way.

Luckily for James, Dad soon rushed into the hallway just outside. Their eyes met. Soon Dad was in the examining room.

"This your father, son?" the deputy asked. James nodded. The deputy looked at Dad. "Deputy Charles Bowie. You?"

"James Daly Sr. His father."

A thin smile crossed the deputy's craggy face. "You've got a smart kid. Knew he didn't want to talk without a lawyer present."

James looked to his father. Surely Dad could get him out of this. "Well, there's a lawyer present now," Dad said with no obvious emotion. He looked at James. "Tell us what happened."

So James did. His father leaned forward, eyes narrow and jaw clenched in the way he did when he was angry, when James revealed that he and his friends had accepted the locals' challenge to a race. The deputy snorted in a way that looked like he was repressing a laugh. The humor drained from his face when James described just where they had been racing.

Then James got to the part about the monster coming out of

the water. "Hold it right there," the deputy interrupted. "You're saying something came out of the water and skewered Bill?" He took another drag on his cigarette. "Something like a big-ass squid?"

James nodded. "Yes sir. It was at least ten feet—"

"There is nothing around here like that," the deputy interrupted. "This isn't California with its giant octopuses."

Outrage welled up within James. He'd figured that part of the story would be hard to swallow, but he wasn't prepared for this blatant dismissiveness. "Sir, it was there. It reared at least ten feet out of the water. It had glowing eyes and—"

Bowie raised an eyebrow. "Glowing eyes? Is there any animal in nature that's got glowing eyes?" James wanted to scream. Why the fuck wasn't the man listening? Before he could object, the deputy leaned forward. James could smell the sharp tobacco on his breath. He met the deputy's eyes for a moment before looking away. "Be honest with me, son, Have you been drinking?"

"How about we let him continue?" Dad interrupted.

Bowie glanced back at Dad. "Fine with me."

James continued the story all the way to the end. When he was finished, Bowie sank into a smaller chair across the room and watched him with those unreadable eyes.

"Your story is consistent, I'll give you that." He kept his eyes locked on James. "But I'm sure you'll forgive me for saying it's just a bit tough to believe." He took another drag on his cigarette. His tone wasn't as harsh as before. James almost raised an eyebrow. The deputy had to know more than he was letting on.

The deputy continued. "It seems more likely that you and Bill got into a fight out in the woods and Bill took a swing at you with a knife. I know the boy. He's a hothead, and with his family situation, he's got a lot to be pissed about. Maybe him laying down his ATV and you having to save his punk ass set him off."

"Excuse me," Dad interrupted. "Did the doctor or nurses show you a picture of the wound before they sewed it up?"

Bowie shook his head. "Nope. They show you?"

Dad nodded. He fished his phone out of his pocket. "I spoke to them on the way here. Once they verified that I was his father, they sent me this." An image of the bloody gash on James' left cheek filled the screen. James winced at the sight of the long open wound. That'd leave a scar for sure. "What kind of knife would that kid have to be carrying to cut that shallow *and* that wide? A knife wound would be deeper and narrower."

The deputy turned away from James. "And what would you know about knives?"

"I paid my way through undergrad working at a Longhorn Steakhouse, then interned as a clerk for a public defender and for a prosecutor." The proud shadow of a smile crossed his face. "The skillset's more transferable than you'd think. I know what it looks like when somebody gets cut by a knife. Whatever knife that kid was carrying—if he were carrying at all—wouldn't leave that kind of wound."

The deputy regarded Dad coolly for a long moment before turning back to James. "As I said, Bill swings at you with a knife." James nearly screamed, but the deputy went on. "You push him into the pond and run like hell for your ATV. Maybe you panicked and thought some of the tree branches were arms. I've been to that area before, and it's right spooky. If you're flipping out because that kid took a knife to your face, it'd be even worse."

James was beyond wanting to scream. Now he wanted to throw something at the fat hick. The deputy had his own scenario in mind and didn't want to be confused with the facts! Then his stomach tightened. Or maybe he knew something about just what *it* was and was trying to cover it up? Just like in *Jaws*, or any number of knockoffs since. That possibility was even worse.

"Where's Bill, then?" Dad asked. "My son had to drive quite a bit before coming out of the woods, and Bill still had his ATV. There was time for him to catch up."

The officer shrugged. "Maybe he hit his head and lost consciousness, or got tangled in tree branches under the surface and couldn't get free. We've called in a dive team from Henry County to look around, but if the body came up, the coyotes might've gotten to it."

James scowled. *Bullshit.* Coyotes wouldn't swim into the middle of a pond for a body. Even if they did, they wouldn't be able to totally destroy it. Especially not in the short time since the thing had taken Bill.

Yep. Definitely a cover-up.

———

THE DEPUTY eventually gave up trying to get James to claim Bill had attacked him and let him and Dad leave the hospital. There was a stern warning about not trying to get the others to change their stories, as though James were some goddamn gang-banger who'd lean on witnesses.

The deputy's interrogation paled beside the wrath unleashed by Mom and Dad when they got home. Dad had ridden the whole way in silence, ignoring James' one attempt to make conversation. James knew there was going to be hell to pay. He was right.

"Do you know how goddamn lucky you are you've got a lawyer for a father?" Dad demanded. James sat alone on the brown leather couch in the living room. Mom sat in the patterned chair, while Dad paced like a watchful tiger in front of the white fireplace. Karen had been sent away, but no doubt she'd be able to hear it upstairs. "Who knows what they'd have badgered out of you at the hospital with your face all mangled like that and nobody recording it!"

"I'm telling the truth! Bill and I didn't get into a fight. There was something—"

"Let's get one thing out of the way first," Mom interrupted. "Have you taken any drugs? Lots of the local kids do drugs and since you were hanging out with them—"

James nearly screamed. They'd told him his whole life not to do drugs! He'd always listened, and now, on the worst day of his life, they're acting like he hadn't listened? James sighed. "No! I'm not on any fucking drugs. How the *fuck* could I afford drugs having to give you most of my paycheck?"

"Oh don't bring that up again!" Dad interrupted. "I don't know what the hell happened out there, but none of this would have happened if you hadn't been so stupid as to get into some pissing contest with some idiot kids." He looked straight at James. "When was the last time you drove an ATV, anyway?"

"A couple of years ago, when we visited Uncle Jim's place out in Ala—"

"Fine." He paced the carpet. "Now a kid is probably dead, and you're the most logical suspect. Do you think they're going to let this go just because I talked them into letting me take you home? They'll turn the screws on Maad or Katie—"

"They wouldn't—"

"They would if they were forced to," Mom interrupted. "Maad's parents aren't citizens as far as I know, and how popular do you think a white girl dating an Indian is going to be down here? If the police want them to, they'll claim before you went off on that stupid race you said you were going to kill that boy."

That was something he hadn't thought about. It did seem

like something the hicks around here would do. Even if they couldn't have Maad's family deported, Maad might not know that. Not only would the local jury be quite willing to believe a "carpetbagger" had murdered one of their own, but the deputy was clearly hiding something. If they decided to give up trying to pin the blame on a dead kid who couldn't defend himself and play hardball...

"The main thing that's likely to save your ass is your face and the fact you'd wet yourself." James reddened at the reminder. "That's not something an aggressor does. But even with that, they could claim you attacked Bill, and he knifed you in self-defense. The shock of it caused you to piss yourself before you shoved him into the pond."

"But you said that wasn't—"

"Working at Longhorn's twenty years ago doesn't make me an expert witness in knives. Neither does clerking on the criminal side. That might've worked on that deputy, but it's not going to cut the mustard with a prosecutor and a jury. *Especially* a jury around here that wants to avenge one of its own."

"Why on Earth did you even agree to this stupid race?" Mom demanded. "What made you think this was a good idea?"

James sighed inwardly. What did Mom know? The girls Mom grew up with back in Raleigh or the ones at UNC Chapel Hill when she was in college wouldn't look like cowards if they backed down from a fight. And from what he'd known of Karen's friends, girls his age wouldn't either. This was something she wouldn't understand, and she shouldn't act like she knew better.

He told Mom the same story he told Dad and Bowie. She didn't take it very well.

"James Andrew Daly! I thought you were more mature than this! Looks like I was wrong. You, young man, are grounded for the next three months."

Enough was enough. "Two months," James retorted.

Mom raised her eyebrow. "I wasn't aware you set punishments in this house."

"I turn eighteen in two months." Silence fell. Now James had really done it. In for a penny, in for a pound. "You tell me none of this would have happened if I hadn't agreed to meet up with Bill and his friends for a race. And you know what? You're right." His lips skinned back from his teeth. "But this wouldn't have happened if we'd stayed in Buckhead!"

Mom threw her hands up in the air. "Here we go again. More of this crap." Her eyes locked on his. She leaned forward. "If you move out, how are you going to survive?"

"I can find a job."

"Maybe, maybe not. Where are you going to live? And all 'your' stuff's really ours. You'd be leaving here with just the clothes on your back, without your car, and–"

Dad's gaze fell on Mom. "Andrea." She scowled, but shut up. He turned to James. "Don't be an idiot." He pointed to the wound in his face. "That'll take a while to heal, and my insurance—such as it is—is going to go a long way to help make sure it doesn't scar. And what if it gets infected and a doctor has to clean it out and sew it up? That'll definitely cost you."

He sighed. "Had I known the economy was going to collapse, we wouldn't have moved. But we owe more than this house is worth, so we can't just sell it and move back. We've got to make the best of this until home prices rebound and *this* isn't helping." He sighed. "If it weren't for this, I'd be glad you're actually meeting new people instead of just hanging around with the same three kids when you're not driving back up to Buckhead."

So that was why Dad was so resistant to just selling and moving home. Despite himself, James had to admit that made sense. Pity it took this happening to get him to actually admit it.

He looked at Mom and then back at James. "I agree with your mother. You're still grounded until this blows over, if nothing else to keep you from doing anything that'd look like witness tampering or getting into more trouble." He leaned forward. "You've never given us any reason to distrust you before, but I agree with the deputy that this is pretty far-fetched. Is there anything you're not telling us? Are you *sure* you didn't get into a fight with that kid?"

James sighed. "Yes I'm sure! When he wrecked, I helped pull the ATV off him! If I wanted to fuck with him—"

"James!"

Dad looked at Mom, then James again. "Don't use that word in this house."

"Fine. If I wanted to mess with him, I'd have left him there. He could've gotten out from under the ATV on his own sooner or later."

"And if he had died, you'd have been responsible," Mom added. "I don't know about legally—that's your father's department—but morally..."

James nodded. "Yeah, but I didn't. I stopped to help him and then that, that—" The image of the thing with too many limbs and too many eyes rising from the water roared back into his mind. Once more Bill rose into the air, impaled on the claws tipping the monster's tentacles. Blood everywhere, so much blood.

It hit him then. Bill was dead. Bill was dead because something had come out of the goddamn water and *eaten* him. In front of James. And James was too weak to stop it. He would have if he could. Bill was going to have a kid. That kid now wasn't going to have a dad because—

"That...thing." James managed to force the words from a mouth grown choked. Not as choked as Bill's mouth had been with the claws buried in his chest, filling his mouth with the blood of his mangled lungs.

A tear dripped down his face. James clenched a fist. He didn't cry when the doctors examined him. He didn't cry when that redneck deputy interrogated him. He sure as hell wasn't going to cry now.

Despite his efforts, another tear slid down his face. He inhaled, clearing his nose of the sobbing-snot that was starting to collect. "I didn't kill him," he insisted. "It killed him."

He looked down at his feet on the fancy rug. He wasn't a child. He shouldn't be crying, no matter what. Another tear dripped down his nose and landed on his right thigh.

Someone sat to his right. A quick glance showed it was Mom. She slid an arm around him. "It's all right," she murmured. "You're home safe now."

Despite himself, James let himself sob.

CHAPTER SEVEN

THE CLEARING WHERE THE CONGREGATION MET WAS crowded tonight. Where there were usually only around fifteen or twenty gathered in the circle the lantern light carved from the darkness, now there were nearly thirty. And many looked angry.

Phillip resisted frowning. They were here because of Bill Aiken. They were here because Edington blood had been shed, innocent blood, only two days before.

Well, relatively innocent. He'd gotten a girl in a family way and hadn't to Phillip's knowledge offered to marry her. As the father of a daughter and now a grandfather too, he didn't approve one single, solitary bit. But there was a difference between that and some drunk making it hard for honest men and women to operate their businesses downtown. That hurt all of Edington, not just one family.

He pulled the hood of the cloak that once belonged to a Creek medicine man forward, hiding his face. He emerged from the darkness and held up his hands for silence. The dark muttering vanished immediately.

Phillip allowed himself to smile. This was a lot easier than he'd thought. The smile faded. Appearances could be deceiving. "Brothers and sisters," he called out, voice loud in the quiet. "As always, it is a joy to see so many of you assembled here tonight to worship."

"Praise Him!" many in the crowd responded, almost automatically. That was good. Maybe the congregation wasn't turning mutinous, but it was never a good idea to assume.

"Most of the time we'd begin with a song," Phillip continued. "But I think some changes are in order tonight. Let's start with the concerns of the congregation." Phillip's gaze swept the crowd. There. Standing taller than most of his compatriots was County Attorney Zebulon Redding. His thin lips were pursed. His green eyes, normally cool and collected, burned with anger. "Brother Zebulon?"

He stepped forward between Phillip and the congregation, his every move shaking with energy. Phillip raised an eyebrow as the man drew in a deep breath. "Y'all know that new strip mall going in on the west side?" Phillip almost snorted with disdain. Of course he did! The first new construction in Edington in two years. Everybody in town knew all about that. "Well, in addition to some of our folk they'd hired, they've also brought in some Mexicans."

Unlike some, Phillip didn't have a problem with Mexicans, at least not in large numbers. They were good, hard workers, and family-oriented. They'd left their homes in search of a better life elsewhere and once they'd saved up enough money, most went back to where they came from. Still, he intended to let the other man speak his piece.

"My little girl told me this afternoon that when she's been riding her bike to school past the construction site, some of them have been *leering* at her."

Phillip leaned forward. That's how it would start, with a

look. Then they'd start following her in a van until they had the chance to snatch her without others seeing. He'd heard of similar things before. The dark muttering began again. This time it was directed at someone a bit more deserving.

"I told the man running the site, an Edington man like us, to have a word with them. Maybe in Mexico the age of consent is eleven, but it sure as hell isn't here. But he wouldn't listen. He told me they might look, but they'd *never* touch." His jaw set. His fists clenched at his sides. "That's not a risk I'm willing to take."

Quick as a striking snake, Redding drew a folding knife from his pocket. Out popped the blade, which he laid against the flesh of his right palm. "I don't want some animal ruining my daughter. If it takes my blood to send Him forth, so be it."

Phillip raised an eyebrow. He couldn't argue with a man wanting to protect his daughter from some lowlifes, not easily. But he doubted Redding had done all he could before bringing his concerns to Him. He would want His followers to take responsibility for their own lives rather than immediately begging for His help.

"Brother Zebulon, you are the county attorney. Surely you can arrange for a surprise check on their papers. Might rattle some enough to seek work elsewhere and put the fear of God in the rest."

Redding rolled his eyes. "I'd thought of that. The sheriff said immigration's a federal matter and he doesn't want to tangle with the feds. And even if they get sent back to wherever, what's to stop them from ruining someone else's daughter?" A cold smile split his face. "This way they'll never hurt any children, *ever*."

Phillip nodded. "A fair point. Anyone else?"

John Thomas, still burly despite being a decade older than Phillip, pushed his way to the front. Phillip raised an eyebrow.

He hadn't seen him in the woods in nearly a month. "I've got a concern," the older man began. "I bet I'm not the only one who does."

The elephant in the clearing had just sounded its trumpet. Phillip felt almost relieved. Now was the time to do, or die. "What is this concern, Brother John?"

"Bill Aiken, my great-nephew."

Phillip had to think fast. This was not how things worked. He would kill those who threatened His worshipers' lives, prosperity, or peace of mind. Bill Aiken wasn't a member of the congregation, but he hadn't wronged anybody in it either.

Phillip smiled. "That's a good question." That bought time, but Thomas wasn't the patient sort. The thought of siccing Him on the man bubbled up from the depths of Phillip's brain, but he pushed the thought aside. Feeding Him fellow congregants was almost unheard of. They'd disposed of traitors, of course, but Thomas wasn't one.

An idea occurred to Phillip. This'd get the attention back on the outsiders like the perverts at the construction site or the carpetbaggers where it belonged.

"Bill's blood is on his own head." Thomas's eyes bulged. His huge hands curled into fists. Angry words raced through the assembled worshipers. It was clear they loved their boy more than their god. "Bill should have made an honest woman out of Sarah but instead he burdened her with a bastard. Judgment begins at the house of God." He didn't believe in the Bible he was cribbing from, but most of the congregation at least had some church. That'd resonate.

The muttering subsided but didn't vanish. And Thomas still looked pissed. Fortunately, now came the scapegoating part.

"But although sins must come, woe to him whom through they come!" Phillip shouted. That got some congregants' attention, including Thomas's. "Bill should have married Sarah when he knew. Many of you had been in his shoes before and unlike him, made the right decision. But why did *you*, and not *he*, make the right decision?"

Phillip paused and let his words sink in. "It's the bad influence of the carpetbaggers, that's what. All of us have the sense He gave a turnip to keep filth like that *Sixteen and Pregnant* show where young men fail to take responsibility out of our homes and away from our kids. But the carpetbaggers don't. And their kids influence ours. Sins must come, but woe to him whom through they come!" He paused for effect. "Tell me, brothers and sisters. What punishment is there for those who are stumbling blocks to others?" He searched his memory. He'd been to church to keep up appearances, but his knowledge of the Bible was a bit rusty. "Those who cause others to sin should have a great millstone tied to their necks and thrown into the waters! The dark waters! Where He dwells!"

The worshipers shouted in response, calling for vengeance. Vengeance on the carpetbaggers for leading Bill astray. Vengeance on the perverse Mexicans who thought an eleven-year-old was a woman and not a child.

Vengeance Phillip would soon call on Him to deliver. He turned away and strode beneath the trees to the edge of the dark waters. He knew the gentle deepening of the pond was a deception. Once one got out a ways, the floor dropped away hundreds of feet. Their god dwelt there, a god who could be summoned reliably if one knew just what to do.

He bent downward and drew the slightly curved seven-inch recon knife he'd carried as a young Marine in Vietnam from the sheath on his calf. The lantern light danced across the shiny blade. Though it had shed much blood in the decades since he first went into the jungle, he kept it immaculately clean and sharp.

He set the knife to his palm, on the crosshatch of scar tissue previous summonings had left. He gave the blade a push. The scarring parted beneath the blade like a barbecue roll. Familiar pain lanced up his arm, but long practice kept it from his face. Blood, dark even against the black water, dripped onto the surface of the pond and dissipated.

Phillip waited. Although He had eaten an unexpected meal the other day, something of His size would hunger easily. Phillip had just the target in mind, and it wasn't the Mexicans that so enraged the county attorney.

The water moved, concentric ripples reaching for his feet. Someone else, someone less experienced, might write that off as the movement of some fish, but not Phillip. The grin snaked wider across his face. The water lay still for a moment. Then the water lapped at his feet, licking at the toes of his Army surplus boots like an affectionate dog.

Phillip raised both hands high and shouted loud enough for those in the clearing to hear. "He has heard us!"

Shouts echoed behind him. "He has heard us!"

They weren't nearly as enthusiastic as usual. Now that nobody human could see him, Phillip let himself frown. He knew just what was needed to keep the feelings high.

———

THE FULL MOON watched as Sam's red pickup truck slowly rolled up the long, empty road, lights off and license plate taped over. The Indian family's sturdy two-story house lay ahead on the right just beyond the edge of the great pine forest. Sam drove, with Deputy Bowie in uniform in the front seat. Behind them, crammed into a space more suitable for extra storage than passengers, were Reed and Thomas. Thomas carried a revolver, while Reed bore an AR-15. Overkill for this mission, but it was always better to be overprepared than under-prepared.

Sam inhaled, then exhaled as they pulled up to the side-walk barely in sight of the Indians' well-lit house. Although He could fight His own battles against men doomed to die, it was a great honor to go to war in His name.

The Indian family didn't live far from the tree farm, so they made a logical target. Phil had ordered Sam to go collect them for the sacrifice. It would strengthen his faith and courage, the high priest said.

Sam swallowed. He was a good soldier. He followed the orders of the legitimate authorities. What could be a more legit-imate authority than the god's priest, even if some of his more recent decisions had made him wonder? And it wasn't like he hadn't done anything like this before.

The Indians' home wasn't the only one on this street, but it was the only one with anybody actually living in it. The houses flanking it were empty. Whoever had built them hadn't been able to sell them. Phil said the developers from Atlanta had gone under, done in by their own greed. He'd made sure members of the congregation did their bit keeping the yards mowed and watching for vagrants and copper thieves who might make fine sacrifices to Him. That also kept the congrega-tion informed about who was home, something that turned out real handy just now.

"All right," Reed said. "You all remember the goddamn drill?"

"Yeah," Thomas said. "Bowie brings them here. We put them in the back of the truck."

"Alive," Reed emphasized. "The cow-fuckers must be given to Him *alive*."

"Got it."

Reed looked from Bowie to Sam. "I reckon you two actually

know what you're doing." He fixed his gaze on Sam. "Snatch and grab, that's what they call these kind of missions. Right?"

Sam nodded. Of course, it was all too easy for those types of missions to go to hell. He hadn't been in Mogadishu when the attempt to snatch the warlord who'd stolen the poor folk's food had gone wrong, but he had friends who had. Yep, that one had *definitely* gone wrong.

"Good. Bowie, get them out here."

Bowie nodded before climbing out and making his way across the Indian family's big green yard to the front door.

Sam watched him, but with every step the deputy took toward the house, his own doubts grew. Bill Aiken had put Sarah in a bad way, but that was something that happened a lot in Edington. Nobody had ever been *sacrificed* for that.

And what had the Indian boy and his family done? Sam remembered Indians—Pakistanis, close enough—from when he'd been in the Gulf. They seemed harmless enough, more wronged by their rich Arab employers than wronging anyone else. Their government backed the terrorists, sure, but it wasn't the ones over here that were doing it. He had kin at Edington High School. If that Indian boy was mistreating his girlfriend, he'd know about it, and He would have a new meal.

Bowie ascended the brick steps and rang the doorbell.

"Please don't be home," Sam found himself whispering.

"What?" Reed demanded. "What're you saying?" For a moment, Sam didn't have anything to say. If he told the truth, they'd know him for a traitor and kill him. But he'd always been a bad liar. "Well?"

"I was praying," Sam said, trying to sound as pious as possible. "Praying that justice be done upon the bad folk in the world."

Thomas laughed. "Isn't that a good prayer? Who do you think deserves it more, a bunch of curry-eaters or some spics lusting after a little girl? I'm thinking it's the Mexicans myself, but—"

Reed's gaze snapped back toward the deputy, but that didn't shut him up. "Who knows if those pathetic spics will ever actually do anything?" Reed scowled. "Not that I want them to molest Brother Zebulon's daughter, mind, but I'm willing to bet this one's already done the deed with that stupid girl."

Sam ignored Reed's ranting and watched Bowie. An Indian woman with gray beginning to streak her dark hair dressed all pretty in blue trimmed with gold stood in the doorway. Bowie was holding up his badge, but she wasn't coming out.

Why wasn't he bringing the whole family down to the truck? What was taking him so long? Sam hadn't expected the Indian family to resist.

"Goddamn it," Reed snarled. He pulled the black ski mask from his pocket. "This is taking too damn long. Brother John, mask up. Brother Sam, stay here and be ready to drive."

What the hell were they doing? Bowie was a sheriff's deputy and the Indian family might not know in this country they actually had rights. Maybe he wanted to try a soft approach rather than strong-arming the Indians out of their stout house.

"Brother Jeffrey—" Sam began. Reed silenced him with a glare.

"They're used to being slaves. It won't take much to scare them out here."

Reed banged the door open, holding onto his AR-15 with one hand. Thomas followed after. His revolver was still in its holster, but someone of his size didn't really need a gun to subdue the unarmed.

"Wait!" Sam called out. "You'll ruin—"

He clamped his mouth shut. If the Indian woman actually

saw the two masked men heading their way, all hell could break loose.

And that was exactly what happened. Both Bowie and the woman looked toward the car. While the big deputy's head was turned, the Indian woman retreated into the house and slammed the door behind her.

Bowie pounded on the door. Reed raised his rifle as he approached the house, gaze locked on the windows. Sam's mind raced. Did Indians like to own guns? If they did, things were about to go south like they had at Mogadishu.

Bowie retreated, drawing his service pistol and pulling back his foot. A lot of the new houses in town weren't built that well. A good kick might break the lock and—

CRACK! Glass exploded outward from the window to the right of the front door. And that was only the first gunshot. Another soon followed. Bowie threw himself down the red-brick stoop onto the cement path that crept alongside the house.

CRACK-CRACK-CRACK. Three round burst. Reed had never served in the military as far as Sam knew, but he had good fire discipline. Windows shattered. Someone screamed. Bowie scrambled back down the yard, the knees of his uniform pants torn and bloody. Once he was close to the street, he rolled over and aimed his gun at the door.

Suddenly sirens began wailing like the banshees in Grandma's scare-stories. As the seconds passed, they didn't fade out as they ought. This was unincorporated county land. The Sheriff's Office would know not to interfere with His business.

Blue lights flashed in the distant darkness well ahead of the truck. Whoever it was out there didn't look like they were going elsewhere. Sam's hands trembled on the wheel. They'd covered his license plate for the mission, but there weren't so many red pickup trucks in Edington he'd wager his freedom on the police not recognizing his.

He turned the key in the ignition. The engine thundered, nearly drowning out another gunshot from inside the house. Whatever his fire discipline, Reed hadn't actually hit whoever was shooting.

Where was He? The four men were going to collect sacrifices for Him. The oncoming police shouldn't be a problem for a god. Sam looked behind him toward the road leading to the tree farm. Nothing stirred in the darkness beyond the taillights. He wasn't coming.

Sam's eyes returned to the blue lights in the distance. They grew brighter each passing second. The congregants were definitely going to have company soon.

Sam blew the horn. Thomas, closest to the truck, took the hint and raced back. "Into the bed!" Sam shouted. There wasn't time for anybody to get in the cab. "Get down!" Sam threw the truck into reverse, driving quickly enough to get out of sight but not fast enough the others couldn't catch up.

Never leave a man behind.

"Hey!" Reed shouted. "Where the hell are you going?"

Sam wheeled down the window. "The bed!" he screamed. "Get in the truck bed!"

Another gunshot from within the house emphasized his point. Reed turned and fired a burst straight through the door before he and Bowie raced away from the house. No gunshots followed. As soon as they'd jumped in the truck bed, Sam floored the accelerator. The truck shot backward the way it came. Sam shut off the headlights, but as he pulled back, he got a brief glimpse of the police cars coming around the corner down the street from the house.

It was the Edington Police Department. There were brother congregants in it, but not many. Unlike the Sheriff's

Office, they couldn't be trusted to not investigate the congregation's doings.

"Shit!" he swore. They had to get out of there *now*. Sam threw the truck into drive and U-turned through a vacant house's yard. They'd get the hell out of there, find some quiet place to get the tape off the license plate, and make their way back to the tree farm. There'd be no sacrifice tonight, but they wouldn't have risked the congregation's OpSec either.

It wasn't long before blue lights flashed in his rear-view mirror. Sam's heart leaped into his throat. They were in deep shit now.

"Damn it!" Reed snarled through the open back window. "Sam, fucking *drive*!"

Sam doubted his old truck could outrun a police cruiser, especially with those new ones the department had bought with the federal stimulus money. They were in a right pickle now, and it'd take a miracle to get them out.

He whispered under his breath, calling on Him for aid. The god of the woods could smash a police cruiser as effortlessly as a TOW rocket could shatter one of the Iraqis' second-rate tanks. Easier than that, in fact. Hundreds had died fighting Saddam Hussein, but nobody could hurt a god.

The truck rocketed down the dark road, the police cruiser close behind. A second pair of lights whirled behind the first. Now the sirens were howling in the dark night. Sam's headlights illuminated the curving country road ahead, the forests pressing against the pavement. It would be awhile before they could find an intersection or another place to turn off. And the longer the chase went on, the more likely the police would head them off.

A gunshot popped from the truck bed behind him. It sounded like a revolver. Sam's gaze snapped back. Somebody—probably John—was actually *shooting at the police!*

"Stop!" Sam demanded, urgency boiling in his voice.

"Why?" Reed demanded. "It gets these bastards off our ass!"

"Brother John's gun is something he bought legally, right?"

Reed shrugged. "As far as I know."

Sam nearly screamed. "They find bullets, they'll be able to trace them! They'll send the EPD right to his house!"

That got Reed's attention. "Shit, man." He turned to John. "Cut that the fuck out!" he demanded.

There were no more gunshots. Sam's gaze jumped back up to the rearview mirror. Both police cruisers kept coming. Sam allowed himself to sigh in relief. He didn't know how he could live with himself if they actually hurt or killed a cop. He hoped the bullet was buried in a tree or the mud where it'd never be found.

Where was He? Surely He would know they were fighting in His name and help them emerge victorious? Even though they'd failed to get the sacrifice, their arrest would put His worshippers in danger.

Reed stuck his head through the back window. "Brother Sam, they're still coming." For the first time, he actually sounded frightened. "If we can't shoot them, what the hell are we supposed to do?"

Sam wanted to tell Reed to have faith in Him. The one who'd protected Edington from the soldiers over a century ago would surely protect His warriors. But as the police cars continued nipping at their heels, He did not come. A lump rose in Sam's throat. Could He not extend His power beyond his lair?

The truck bounced as it hit what must've been a pothole. Sam immediately looked back up at their pursuers. Were his eyes playing tricks on him, or was that a third police cruiser behind them? How were they going to get out of this pickle?

His gaze flickered over to the dashboard. The burning red triangle of the hazard light button sat there clear as day. He swallowed. He didn't want to hurt the police. But he didn't want to be arrested and get the congregation into trouble neither. He wasn't coming to help His folk. So Sam would have to get them out of this situation all by his lonesome.

"Brother Jeffrey! The hazard lights!"

Reed grinned. "Great idea!" The big man reached past Sam and jammed a thick finger down on the red rectangular button.

Red lights blazed behind them. The police cruisers immediately fell back with the screaming of brakes. Metal crunched a second later as the trailing police car slammed into the first. Sam winced. Hopefully those were the brand-new cars. Those would have the most effective airbags.

He floored the accelerator. The police cars vanished behind them. Once a minute had passed, and they hadn't reappeared, he dialed down the headlights as low as they'd go and still light the way ahead. They'd have to find somewhere to hide and wait for the police to start looking for them elsewhere.

———

PHILLIP HAD ALREADY SMASHED A SAPLING FLAT into the mud with his booted foot, but his rage still hadn't been expended. Not only had the raiding party he'd sent out *not* brought back the Indian family for sacrifice, but they'd gotten into a gunfight and had to fucking beat feet from the Edington police! They'd returned safe and sound after evading the cops and laagering up in a field with their lights off for an hour, but this was still an intolerable fuckup!

For a moment he considered cutting Reed's throat himself. Reed was younger and stronger, but he wouldn't expect this.

The authority Phillip had as the leader of the congregation should keep him from fighting back. That would show everyone the price of failure, especially when the stakes were this high.

He looked back through the brush tangled amidst the trees into the center of the lantern light where the congregants gathered. The muttering was loud even a dozen yards away. Phillip bet there were congregants already wondering if they should turn traitor, buying mercy from the law that would surely come down on them now. The congregation might fail this very night, all thanks to Reed.

Phillip shook his head. Reed was an idiot, but command responsibility was ultimately on his shoulders. *He* should have remembered that the area had been annexed by the carpetbagger-influenced city and they'd put a police substation in that half-vacant strip mall nearby. *He* should have realized Reed was an impatient ass and might FUBAR a mission requiring delicacy.

Still, Reed would have a part to play in the drama that would help keep order in the congregation. Phillip turned to face the brute.

"Brother Jeffrey, ring the bell."

Reed walked toward the pair of gnarled black wood posts holding up the ancient iron bell the very first settlers had made for the Creeks not knowing its holy purpose. He was halfway to the bell before he stopped abruptly.

"Sir, we don't have a sacrifice."

"He is waiting, Brother Jeffrey. Do you wish to disappoint Him?"

Reed quickly shook his head. Phillip turned toward the assembled worshipers. This was the first time he could remember where they'd failed to capture a sacrifice for Him. It would be better if they could run out and kidnap some random vagrant. But that would take time they didn't have, even if they could find one. There hadn't been a lot of homeless downtown lately. The irony almost made him smile. Offering Tolliver to Him wasn't just to get rid of one vagrant, but to put the fear of Him into the rest. They'd succeeded, all too well.

It looked like they'd have to offer up one of their own. Phillip caught Reed in the corner of his eye. The man had fucked up the night's raid and then had the gall to question his authority. That couldn't be tolerated. But even if he was a dumb hothead, he was an excellent enforcer, never showing any reluctance to do what was necessary for the congregation and for Edington. Nope. He was too useful.

Then Phillip's gaze fell on Sam. The Army puke was weak. He'd also questioned his authority, in his own restaurant no less. And now, even deep within the tree farm outside of the jurisdiction of a police department infested by carpetbaggers, he looked frightened. If he went around scared of his own shadow, folk would start asking questions. The congregation didn't need that. Not now. Sam knew too much, and he might talk.

No. He was a veteran, a man who put his life on the line for his kin and nation. Phillip had given the order to put Tolliver out of his misery, but Tolliver was a pathetic wreck. Sam was salvageable. And he was married to his cousin's stepdaughter, who'd suffered enough lately. And he'd also gotten all four raiders back rather than leave them for the Edington cops, who'd make them talk sooner or later. Phillip shook his head. *Not tonight.*

Phillip's gaze fell on Thomas. The big man would do nicely. He'd dared challenge the will of the god of the woods before the congregation and then gone on a failed mission. His judgment would be clear to all. Discipline would be restored, for the moment at least.

"Brother John." His mild tone disguised lethal intent. "Come forward." The congregation fell instantly silent. Phillip almost smiled. They knew what was going to happen, and it didn't seem like anyone objected. The big man didn't move. "Brother John, I'm waiting."

Thomas hesitantly stepped to the front of the crowd, but he didn't leave it. "Brother Phillip, wh...what are you trying to pull?" Fear writhed in his voice. The hands that had once looked likely to smash Phillip's face trembled.

Phillip ignored the sacrifice-to-be for the moment. "Brother Jeffrey, ring the bell."

Reed looked from Thomas to Phillip, then back to Thomas. Apprehension tickled at Phillip's gut. There'd never been a mutiny in the congregation before, but there was a first time for everything. If Reed joined Thomas in insurrection, it might be *him* going alive into His mouth.

"Brother Jeffrey!" Thomas called out. "You were there! You know we only fled because there were Edington cops there, and more coming!"

Reed reddened. Phillip almost smiled. Bad move, bringing up their defeat like that. Reed turned away from Thomas and seized the rope in his hands. The bell rolled like a crack of thunder, once, twice, three times.

Thomas screamed and tried to flee the circle of light. His bulk made him slow. He barely made it three steps before the others swarmed him and forced him to the wet ground.

"Judgment begins at the house of God!" Phillip called out, again pillaging the Bible. "Let it not be said that we have tried to spare our own!"

"Stop it!" Thomas screamed as they bore him to the blood-stained picnic table, the last stop on the human-sacrifice express for decades. "I'm one of you! I've never sinned against Him!"

Phillip wondered if he should have Thomas gagged. His words might sow seeds of future trouble, seeds that could sprout this very night. Many congregants had firearms and knew how to use them. Hell, Thomas was armed even if he seemed to have forgotten that. Phillip's own gun hung heavily on his hip, but he couldn't just shoot likely troublemakers. He'd only know who he couldn't trust if they'd tried to frag him and failed.

On the other hand, having them shove Thomas's socks in his wide mouth would show the congregation he feared what the man had to say. And showing that would be like showing his pulsing throat to a hungry feral dog. Phillip shook his head. Like hell.

"*All* have sinned," Phillip intoned. "Have you ever watched carpetbagger filth on television or the Internet? Or perhaps dropped hints of just what you've been doing here at night to someone who hasn't been initiated?" *Or maybe gone to Shane's when you could have come to* me *or at least some other local restaurant?*

"No!" Thomas screamed. "No, I swear!" The worshipers tore his clothes away, revealing civvie fat even the Crucible would have problems burning off. Phillip was glad gods didn't have to worry about heart disease.

"Let Him be the judge of that. Your failure tonight was His indictment. Whether He takes you tonight will be the verdict and the sentence."

"The verdict and the sentence!" someone shouted.

With strength no doubt driven by fear, Thomas surged up naked from the table like a pallid missile. One man tried to grab hold of his shoulder, but a blow from a big fist toppled him. Thomas raced across the grassy clearing toward Phillip, eyes wild with fear and rage. Phillip's hand slid inside his robes to his holstered pistol. He'd shoot the big man if he had to, but it would take a sacrifice to truly restore discipline.

He spared a glance behind him. The dark water lapped at the shores of the pond, each little wave wetting the ground farther than the last. Azure lights glowed in the deep. He was coming. Perhaps he should step aside and let Him handle Thomas?

Thomas didn't run fast enough for that to be an option. He'd only gotten a few feet before the congregation forced him to the ground. They bore him back to the table. Thomas thrashed and kicked and swore. A sharp blow to the head stilled his struggling.

"Tie him tightly!" Phillip ordered. "He must not be denied!"

———

THE TOLLING of the great bell had summoned it to feed, as it had in the long years since the Americans had first brought the working of iron to this land. It breached the surface of the dark pond, water draining away from its enormous head. Its long tail forced its vast body through the shallow waters at the edge of the pond into the circle of lights that had once been fiery torches and were now yellow hissing lanterns.

"He comes!" the men shouted at its approach. They spilled out of its way, leaving it a clear path across grass made lush by centuries of blood to its feast. This one was big and pasty, larger than the last one. The dark-skinned offering had been chewy, even when its claws had done their work, and far too small. That wouldn't be a problem this time.

"Please!" the man screamed directly at it. The beast cocked its head, the shadows before it shifting as its glowing eyes moved. Over the long years the offerings had cursed it or the men who'd brought it food or just simply screamed and screamed, but rarely had it been *implored*. It stopped its approach abruptly, watching the bound man.

"Don't kill me! I know we failed to bring You the best prey, those Indians who worship animals and debauch white women, but I'll bring them to you! I swear! Don't eat me and you'll have five of them! Nice, brown morsels fit for you! Fit for a god!"

"Indians." That's what the Americans called the ones who'd brought it food before. But those were gone. No "Istichata" and "Muskogee" had been food or brought it food in a long time. And those had bronze skin, not brown. It wasn't quite sure what the offering was trying to say. Bronze, white, black, brown all tasted the same.

Its enormous maw hinged open, rows of teeth folding forward and locking in place. The man screamed, each cry a distinct breath. It wasn't talking anymore.

The creature's clawed tendrils shot forward. It was time to feed.

———

THOMAS WAS TORN AWAY from the sacrificial table just like Tolliver had been, leaving a hand and foot behind. With a final "PLEASE!" the big man vanished into His cavernous mouth. The rows of sharp teeth meshed together. Bright red blood stained the white enamel. Phillip grinned. Discipline had been restored.

He turned to face his congregation. "He has judged Brother John and found him wanting. But don't think that this makes any of us any better. We have all failed Him!"

"We have all failed Him!" the crowd echoed mournfully.

"But we can do penance!" Phillip called, cribbing from Catholicism this time. The god's feeding tentacles whipped through the air behind him, tearing away what parts of Thomas were left on the table. Phillip couldn't see its glorious feeding, but it no doubt made his speech all the better. "We failed to bring him the meat He requires, but we *will!*"

Phillip turned to face Him, hands raised high. It had slid back into the shallows, its glowing eyes attracting the buzzing denizens of the wet wood like a constellation of bug zappers. It reminded Phillip of the crocodiles he'd seen in Vietnam, sated on the riverside after they'd fed. But crocodiles didn't live forever, didn't survive rifles or even cannon, and wouldn't survive the guns of the police department and the lazy fucks at the National Guard armory if the Edington folk should ever give Him reason to be angry.

"We will not fail you!"

Several of the creature's featureless eyes lazily pivoted his way, their light dying his skin blue-green. Phillip suddenly felt the urgent need to piss. It might amuse onlookers if the sacrifice he'd offered in order to maintain his authority wasn't enough and it ate him next, but *he* wouldn't find it funny. Its gaze held him transfixed like a pinned butterfly. Maybe that was what it was like to be a rabbit caught beneath the eyes of the thousand things that hunted them.

Rather than attack, the creature began receding into the darkness, sinking back into the depths that had vomited it up into the world. Relief flooded through him. The god had not punished him for his sins that day. In fact, by not doing so, He had blessed his leadership of the congregation. Blessed his planned course of action. He watched as the black waters devoured it, only wet black flesh lit by the glowing eyes remaining visible. Those were the last to vanish, disappearing into the depths like the dive lights of a descending frogman.

The waters had not yet returned to normal before Reed approached.

"Sir." There was new respect in his voice. That almost brought a smile to Phillip's face. "Sir, what now?"

"Our brothers in the Sheriff's Office will keep us informed of any interest from law enforcement." Thanks to Reed's stupidity, the congregation was now on the radar of the Edington Police Department. Phillip mentally kicked himself for his carelessness. If he'd fucked up like this in Vietnam, his commanding officer would've ripped him a new one, and he'd have deserved it.

The best-case scenario would be if the police thought his men were robbers bent on stealing the gold he'd heard Indians kept in their homes. That happened often enough where there were more of them. However, he couldn't rely on the police thinking that. The carpetbaggers had to be gotten rid of sooner rather than later, before word of the incident spread. All four, starting with that carpetbagger kid who'd seen Him and escaped. Brother Charles said that one wouldn't do the smart thing and agree that Bill Aiken had tried to kill him. If he talked, folk might come poking around the tree farm. Then more Edington blood would be shed.

The Mexicans could wait. Brother Zebulon should be able to do more than just complain about those incipient child molesters in his position, and they weren't a standing threat to the congregation's OpSec.

No, the carpetbaggers would be the next to go alive into His maw. Although the attempt to capture the Indians had failed, the one who'd defied Him already bore His mark upon his face. They'd get him next.

CHAPTER EIGHT

That Monday was James' next scheduled day at Best Buy. Mom didn't like the idea of him working with his face still bandaged, but Dad pointed out the mortgage didn't care. So after his calculus final, back to work he went. Given how the alternative was spending all the time he wasn't at school in his room without his phone, he didn't mind one single solitary bit.

The day had been a real treat so far. The small-town gossip network had been going full blast. Though Aaron had put him on the shop floor rather than sticking him in the back like he'd hoped, most everybody avoided him. When he sought out customers who looked like they needed help, they somehow never needed it by the time he got there. Aaron ultimately had him scan in returns. That'd keep his bandaged face from frightening the customers.

James could get used to this kind of work. He was still getting paid and wouldn't have to deal with anybody asking about his face or accusing him of homicide with their eyes or gestures, or whispers when they thought he couldn't hear. Or, in the case of one person who must be less prejudiced than the rest of the yokels, flat-out accusing Bill of attempted murder. *Goddamn it!* Bill had actually tried to save him!

He'd just scanned in a couple of shitty chick flicks he bet were unwanted birthday presents when three girls, locals by their accents, breezed in through the out door. The leader of the group was tall and slender with dirty blonde hair.

Amber.

Great. Hopefully she won't be joining the rest of these morons in thinking I murdered Bill, or that Bill tried to murder me.

He stopped suddenly. Why should he care? He looked away from the girls and set the scanned movies on the reshelving cart. Just six more DVDs and one CD—James was shocked anybody was buying CDs these days—and he could get all the returns back on the racks. Then he'd see if Aaron needed help with something. He wouldn't have to deal with Amber and her friends.

"James," Aaron said from behind him. James nearly jumped. He'd been so engrossed in the girls and returns that he hadn't seen his supervisor creeping up on him. Aaron pointed to the three girls. "Go see if they need help."

Great. He needed to keep the job, so he smiled in a way that wasn't too fake and headed over to the trio.

The deep blue eyes of Jessica Johns, a tall brunette with freckles, fell on him before he could even speak. "James," she said with barely-contained disdain. James barely kept from scowling. He didn't know her well, but she'd been much more pleasant before. Her third friend, another brunette who was more than a little bit plump, wasn't as obvious but he could still feel the weight of her eyes.

"So Amber," James said, pretending not to notice the other two girls. "What can I help you with today?"

"I'm looking for a TV for my dorm," Amber said. It just had to be her. Of course, she was actually being pleasant. "Could you show me where the TVs are?"

James looked over his shoulder at the rectangular signs hanging like sharp teeth from the vaulted ceiling. They showed where everything in the store was. Amber had to know how to find the TVs.

"Sure," he said in his best customer service voice. He pointed toward the lines of televisions near the narrow red-lit room reserved for the audio-visual equipment. He led the three over. Amber stuck close to him, while her friends trailed behind. Jessica still watched him warily. James checked the urge to snort. Even if he *had* killed Bill, he wasn't the sort of dickwad who'd hurt a woman.

He showed Amber three different TVs. All were flat-screens, much lighter than the bulky monstrosity he helped his cousin move into her dorm in Tuscaloosa a while back. Amber made all the appropriate comments, but her gaze kept drifting toward the A/V room.

"Are you interested in some speakers to go with that TV?" If that was what she was after, she would get what she wanted and get out of his hair.

"Sure." Her long legs carried her over into the A/V room, leaving James and her friends behind. Not wanting to be left with two hicks who no doubt thought him some kind of city-slicker serial killer, James hurried to catch up.

He wasn't even to the door when Amber looked sternly over his shoulder at her two friends. James' gaze followed hers. The two fell even farther back, although Jessica still looked at him like he was a snake.

"C'mon," she said, urgency breaking into her voice. She looked around the A/V room. James wasn't sure what was going on, but he quickened his pace and soon found himself alone with her.

"All right." Amber fixed her softer blue eyes on him. "Tell me you didn't kill Bill."

"What?" Amber hadn't shared her friends' attitude, so he'd thought she didn't share their suspicions. He'd assumed she just wanted an excuse for some alone time. *Never assume*, he reminded himself. *It makes an ass out of you and me.* "Of course I didn't! If I did, do you think I'd be here?"

"Good." She looked out the doorway at her friends. "That's not what some folk have been saying. Jessica said—"

James rolled his eyes. What did Jessica know? She wasn't there. She hadn't seen that God-knows-what boiling out of the pond, with too many limbs and eyes and teeth. She hadn't seen Bill fucking crucified with claws through his chest.

Amber touched his arm, jolting him back to reality. "James?" she asked. "You just went away there for a second."

James shook his head. "Just remembering."

Amber looked at him, eyes wide in the oval of her face. "Remembering what? Jessica said Deputy Richards said—"

James froze. The deputy who'd interrogated him was named Bowie, but there were three others at the hospital. "The deputies've been talking?"

"Everybody talks around here, especially folk who shouldn't. Figured you'd have realized that by now."

"Great. Just great."

James looked at the two girls outside, who were now looking at their watches. A small smile kinked his face. No matter how long he kept them waiting, he could justify it by saying Amber wanted to discuss A/V equipment. Wasn't the customer always right?

"You want to know what happened out there in the woods?" He paused. "I'll tell you. But not now." He looked at the two girls. "You never know who might be listening." He wondered where Amber might like to meet. The coffee shop where his sister hung out and her friends? No. He wouldn't want Karen to catch him there with Amber. She'd never let him forget it. "My shift tomorrow starts a bit later than I thought. How about the Baskin and Robbins over by the cemetery after school?"

Amber smiled. "I'd love to."

James looked back at the two other girls. They'd been cautious earlier, but now they just looked bored. James was sure to raise his voice. "Do you need help with anything else?"

Amber smiled. "I think I've got all I came for. Thanks for your help."

He watched her walk away with her friends before stepping out of the A/V room. He'd barely gotten out of the door before a sudden whisper from his left stopped him dead in his tracks.

"Hey!" Based on the accent, it must be one of the locals. James' head snapped to the left. Did Amber have a boyfriend? It'd be just like some of the kids around here to pick a fight over that, "murderer" or not.

It wasn't some jealous local. It was Sam, the film buff he'd helped the other day. James doubted he'd have come to the Best Buy just to harass him. James put his big fake customer service grin back on. "Can I help you?"

"I need to tell you something."

A fearful tingling passed over James' scalp. He looked around. "Sir," James said, turning up his best customer-service voice as high as it went. "My supervisor had me scanning in some returns before sending me to help some other customers and I need to get back to that. But I can get someone else who can—"

Sam rolled his eyes. "Don't start that customer service bullshit with me, son." He sounded an awful lot like a drill sergeant. "The other day I bought *Borat* and I decided I want some new speakers to experience it properly. Can you help me pick them out?"

James sighed. The customer was always right. Or at least that's what he'd throw at Aaron if he got upset he'd left the returns on the cart. This guy might know more about what was going on. "All right, sir." He couldn't sound less enthusiastic. Even if the man knew something, James still didn't want to end up alone with some strange redneck.

Sam's long stride carried him past James into the A/V room. James hung back by the door. Whatever Sam intended would be hard for anybody to see from outside unless they were already watching like Amber's friends had. On the other hand, he'd be an idiot to try something in public with dozens of customers between him and the door. And he probably did know something about whatever was going on.

"What can I help you with?" James asked, letting the pretense drag on a bit longer.

Sam examined a big, blocky subwoofer, seeming for all the world like a prospective buyer. But then he opened his mouth. "All right. Let's get down to brass tacks. I know Bill Aiken didn't take his pocketknife to your face."

How the hell did he know what the deputy's bullshit cover story was? "I...I don't know what you're talking about."

Sam sighed. "I know he didn't take his knife to your face because I've seen what *really* did"—he pointed to the bandage— "that."

Fear began a slow march up James' back like an inchworm made of ice. His gaze darted to the door. How long would it take him to get out of the room, get into the store with the other customers? This crazy hick wouldn't *dare* do anything to him in front of so many people.

"Seen what?"

Sam sighed. "Stop playing dumb with me. It's got a lot of arms, eyes that glow, and lives—mostly—in that tree farm."

James looked at the door again. It was only ten feet, fifteen at the most. Hell, even if Sam tackled him, he could scream that the man wanted to rape him. That'd get the good people of Edington up in arms. A man trying to molest a kid, that'd score no points with the people around here *at all*.

But this man knew what had happened the other day. The deputy who'd interrogated him had known something, but persisted with that bullshit story. Not only that, but he'd gotten the small-town gossip network in on it too. If Sam was willing to break the redneck code of silence, maybe he should listen.

James sighed. "All right. What the hell is going on?"

Sam looked around, as though he expected someone to eavesdrop. "It's been here since before the white men came. The Indians who'd built the mounds worshiped it. When the diseases killed them, the Creek who came afterward took it up." He swallowed. "The soldiers learned not to poke around, leaving some Indians behind even when the rest went to Oklahoma. Then the settlers came in and learned just why it was that these Creeks didn't get rounded up."

Gears turned in James' mind. "It killed the soldiers who'd come to put the Indians on the Trail of Tears, and when the settlers killed the Indians, it took revenge."

"Yep. We learned to feed it like the Indians did. Animals, or folk we didn't like. Slaves learned real quick not to run away."

Cold sweat began beading under James' brow. Slaves in most places could expect whippings, brandings, or being sold somewhere worse if they misbehaved. Here, troublesome slaves had become *food*.

At least if Sam wasn't pulling all this out of his ass. Even though he'd seen *something* shove claws through Bill Aiken's chest and swallow him whole, his rational mind rebelled at the idea of generations of Indians and rednecks worshiping a tentacle monster. This was real life, not some 1980s horror movie. All Sam needed to do was start screaming "outlander," and it'd be perfect.

Still, part of him wanted to know more.

"When the War came, most men went off to fight," Sam continued. "Eventually the government sent for more, but the Milledgeville boys didn't come back. They claimed there were Union men responsible, but never sent in the Home Guard to root them out like they did elsewhere. They'd learned to stay well enough away."

James found himself nodding. Freedom from the Confederate draft, in exchange for the lives of the draft men. From what he'd studied in school about Gettysburg or Antietam, not a bad bargain to make.

He shook his head suddenly. Was he believing this man? Sam kept on talking, oblivious to James' growing skepticism.

"And no slaves ran away during the war neither, even when Sherman came close. The men he'd sent—"

James raised his hands. "Hold it. Hold it right there. People were disappearing around here, and *nobody* noticed?"

"It was war." Sam sighed. "Look, if you don't believe me, run down to the library. Go get *Civil War Mysteries* and look up what happened to the men from the 12th Missouri. They fought for the Union at Lovejoy Station before coming here. They ran the Home Guard to ground in the woods east of town but didn't come out of the forest alive. Do you think a bunch of old men, boys, and slavers' sons could defeat the men who'd taken Atlanta?"

He took James' hand and pressed a piece of paper into it.

"Read it," he repeated. "Then call me. You see your Indian friend lately?"

A chill rolled up James' spine. Maad hadn't been at school that day. Someone had said something about an attempted robbery at Maad's house, but James had called Maad and gotten only voicemail. Given Maad's neighborhood, it seemed more likely that someone had gotten caught breaking into an empty house for the metal, Maad had been home sick, and someone put two and two together. The way people gossiped around here, that would be the simplest, most probable situation.

That didn't seem to be the case anymore.

"What happened to Maad?" James demanded.

"Nothing. Nothing yet. But somebody tried." Sam swallowed. "Four somebodies. One of them being me."

James looked back toward the door. There were people outside. He could run, get out of the room into the store where this racist shithead wouldn't dare attack him.

Sam grabbed his arm. James snapped his arm down out of the older man's grasp, pushing apart the thumb and fingers the way his Choi Kwong Do teacher taught so long ago. He followed up with a swing straight for the goddamned redneck's nose. Stun, then run.

Sam blocked the swing with his forearm. "Listen!" he hissed. "I'm through with that. No more. Your friend and his girl did nothing wrong. Neither did Bill. And yet that, that *thing* killed Bill, and Phil sent us—"

"Who the hell is Phil?" Sam clammed up immediately. James sighed. "Never mind. Sent you to do what?"

"Sent us to take the witnesses to Him for sacrifice. They don't care about Bill's friends, but they do care about you and yours."

"Wait a second. The sheriff's deputies could have made us all disappear last weekend. Why didn't they?"

"Not every deputy's in the congregation, and some'll hesitate if they're sent after someone who'll be missed. But they're moving now." He paused. "Read that book. And then call me."

He abruptly turned and left. James looked down to the paper in his palm. It was a piece of copy paper with a phone number scrawled on it. He grit his teeth. He should throw it away and be done with it. He only had a couple more months stuck in this crazy place. Then he could get the hell out.

But then he'd never learn just what the hell was going on. Was there really some monster in the woods eating people? For hundreds of years? That couldn't possibly be true.

His hand drifted back to the bandage across his face. Could it?

Slowly, he slid the paper into his pocket.

———

"So," Ellen Martin said from across the black chain-link table. "You still think he didn't do it?"

After their excursion to the Best Buy, the three had crossed Fayetteville Boulevard to the Happy Cow, the new shop where one could buy frozen yogurt by the ounce. The trio sat at the table outside, the striped canopy keeping the May sun at bay.

Amber's gaze fell to her vanilla frozen yogurt liberally festooned with cookie dough. A twinge of guilt about her faster metabolism crossed her mind as she compared her dessert to her heavier friend's smaller and simpler portion.

But something far darker than guilt lurked deep in her mind. She had a darn good idea who—or more accurately, what —had killed Bill and marred James' freckled face. But she dared not tell her friends her suspicions. Who knew who might be listening, or who they might tell? She didn't want to have visitors in the night just like—

No. Stop that right now.

"Ellen, if the sheriff really thought he'd done it, why isn't he in jail?"

"Deputy Richards said his daddy was with him," Jessica added helpfully. "Giving him advice. Keeping him out of trouble."

"Deputy Richards wasn't there," Amber retorted. "He was questioning Katie—"

Jessica rolled her eyes. "Katie Wallace. Can you believe she's still dating Maad? Even going to *Tech* with him? I mean, he's—"

"Jessica, quit it. Nothing's wrong with Maad. In fact, he came pretty close to being the Minstrel in the play."

Jessica shrugged and returned to her yogurt. "I'm just *saying*. Deputy Richards *said* Katie *said* James drove out of the woods muddy and bloody, just like if he'd gotten into a fight."

Or barely escaped something else.

"Amber, do you really think Bill tried to kill him?" Ellen said. "I mean, if Bill really wanted to, he wouldn't need to go to all the trouble of racing him first." She paused. "I know you like him and all, but that doesn't mean he's a good person. At all."

Amber reddened. A scowl soon complemented the red on her face. "Oh, I know that." Her last boyfriend had been handsome and was even being scouted for soccer scholarships as a sophomore. And then she caught him under the bleachers with her best friend. Her *then* best friend. And that hadn't been his first sin.

"If Bill didn't try to kill him and he didn't kill Bill, what happened?" Jessica asked.

Amber had to think quickly. If she let her suspicions air, not only was she putting herself in danger but she was risking

James' safety too. If they thought he was blabbing all over town, threatening to reveal their dirty little secret...

"You remember that circus that got closed down in Fayetteville last year?" The other two girls nodded. "Well, I heard they lost a couple animals. Big cats. Maybe one or two made it down here, and that was what attacked them."

Ellen nodded. "Makes sense. There're plenty of deer and turkeys hereabouts."

The conversation soon shifted gears to the more prosaic subjects Amber had little interest in. She ate her yogurt and contributed just enough to be polite, but her mind was on her upcoming meeting with James. She'd like to call it a date, but it wasn't a date.

She almost sighed.

———

When his shift was over, rather than going straight home like he was supposed to, James headed down Fairmont Street toward the red brick Edington Branch Library. A wise man had once said, "Trust but verify," and given what had attacked him that Saturday in the woods, being skeptical right now struck him as really fucking stupid.

When he got there, he plopped himself in front of a surprisingly modern computer at a weathered desk and typed in the number of the library card Mom insisted he get. Sure enough, the library had *Civil War Mysteries* and it was in the oooo section.

Just as expected. When he was in the fourth grade he'd gone through a Bigfoot phase and that was where the Bigfoot books were, along with the UFOs and conspiracy theories. For a moment he wondered if the thing he saw was a cryptid. Maybe the locals were worshiping some kind of Loch Ness

Monster? There obviously wouldn't be just one—even turtles only lived for around a century or so—but that would explain it. The Edington Plesiosaur? The Edington Monster Squid? He shook his head. If it were that mundane, someone around here would have had it up on his wall next to the deer heads by now.

Finding the book wasn't that hard. The jacket was gray with blue letters. The binding had eroded at the corners. It didn't look like it had been checked out or even moved in years. Dust came with it when he pulled it free.

The springs of the comfortable burgundy chair in the corner by the magazine rack squeaked as he settled in. He hoped he hadn't broken anything. He didn't need a huge library fine on top of everything else. He opened to the table of contents and looked for the chapter Sam told him about.

The 12th Missouri Volunteer Infantry were part of a force chasing General Hood's Confederates into Alabama after the fall of Atlanta. While moving south and west, they'd sent a mounted foraging party toward Edington. They'd broken a group of Home Guard on the road north of town and pursued them into "a wet wood." The men never returned. After the war, a soldier barely more than a skeleton claiming to have been with the unit was found at the Confederate prison in Andersonville. All he would say about what had taken his companions was "the thing in the woods." He'd died soon afterward. No investigation of the missing soldiers was ever made.

"Well shit." James immediately realized he'd just said it out loud, in the quiet of the library. An old lady sitting in another one of the purple chairs fixed him with a disapproving glare from behind an issue of Cat Fancy. He turned red. "Sorry."

He thought back to the ATV race, to the dark, wet woods. He'd come in on an ATV rather than horseback. And when the thing came, he could outrun it. The Union soldiers only had their two feet or their panicking horses. They'd died horribly in the damp and dark, eaten alive by a monster—

"Well, well, well, what do we have here?" someone else's voice intruded. James nearly jumped out the chair. Karen stood there in front of him, her backpack hanging off her shoulder and what could easily be described as "a shit-eating grin" across her wide face. "Somebody should be in his room when he's not at school or work."

James had a ready answer for that. "I'm supposed to be at home and when I'm not at work or at *school*." He gestured toward her with the book. "This is a history book. This is for school." He smiled back, deliberately mimicking her expression as much as possible.

Karen shook her head. "Nice try. You took U.S. History as a junior before we even moved here. That's not for school."

James looked over his shoulder. There were too many people in the library. How was he supposed to explain this without someone dangerous listening in? If Sam were right, there could be a lot of unfriendly ears out there.

"All right," James said. "Amber asked me to—" He realized he'd said "Amber" and not "Sam" a second too late. Karen wouldn't know who Sam was, but she sure as hell knew Amber.

Karen started laughing. James' ears burned. He looked around. The old lady was fortunately still too engrossed in her magazine to notice. Karen managed to slow down long enough to actually speak. "Amber? Took you long enough!"

James reddened even more. "Amber wanted me to read something in one of these books before we meet up for ice cream tomorrow. Don't tell Mom and Dad."

Karen laughed. "Oh don't worry, I won't." Her grin widened. "If you take out the trash for me the next two months."

James sighed. So much for sibling solidarity. "Fine."

Karen smiled. "That's a good brother. You two have fun."

She walked away before James thought to warn her that he was in danger and that meant she could be too. He looked at his watch. It didn't always take the same amount of time to get from work, but he was pushing the envelope in terms of what he could explain away by claiming traffic.

He put the book away and scuttled out of the library.

CHAPTER NINE

"YOU'RE SAYING YOUR DAD GOT SHOT BY A *SHERIFF'S* deputy?" James asked. He immediately shut his mouth. The Edington High School cafeteria was loud and crowded during fourth-period lunch, but his voice carried.

Maad had returned to school that day, less than twenty-four hours after Sam's warning. Despite that, James still suspected what he'd heard about a break-in was nothing more than small-town gossip. But what Maad had told him when they sat at their customary table in the cafeteria corner near the vending machines changed things.

A sheriff's deputy had asked for the family to come outside, but only offered the vaguest reason. Then his mother had spotted the masked men and slammed the door. Maad's father had recently bought a gun and started shooting. Though he'd driven the mysterious attackers away, a ricocheting bullet to the leg put him in the hospital.

Maad shook his head. "If that were the case, he would be in jail right now. The Edington police suspect it was some hooligan wearing a uniform he bought or stole. A real deputy wouldn't have masked men with him."

Part of James wanted to believe Maad's explanation. There were stores where somebody could buy uniforms. Movie companies did it all the time. Some local thug must've bought one, but couldn't afford more for his posse. He'd use that to get Maad's family under control so his goons could ransack the house. Meth-heads, probably. Just because they were rotting their brains and teeth didn't mean they were stupid.

But the sensible answer wasn't always the right one. James' hand rose unconsciously toward his still-bandaged left cheek. The deputy tried to convince him that some tentacle monster hadn't attacked him in the woods, that Bill had gotten angry and knifed him. And now a man in a deputy's uniform tried to kidnap Maad's family.

Fear rippled through James. That lined up very nicely with what Sam had told him at Best Buy. Was one of the masked men Sam? Or did he drive the getaway car?

James looked around the teeming cafeteria, at the dozens of students gathered beneath the looming central tree. Nobody around them seemed to be paying attention, but all it would take is one person talking. Knowing Edington, someone would. Word would get back to the Sheriff's Office and they'd try for Maad, him, or perhaps even both.

"Okay, we've got to be careful about this," James said quickly. "I'm really not supposed to be talking to you in the first place, but if they hear I've been talking to you about *this*, I'll get in even more trouble." Maad nodded. "What is your family doing?"

"Dad's at home now, on crutches." He frowned. "They took his gun away 'for evidence.' What are we supposed to do if those hooligans come back? The police say they'll run patrols by our house, but we're still pretty far from Edington even if we're still in the city limits."

Would the cultists go after Maad's family again soon, or would they wait for the heat to die down first? James frowned. There was only one person he knew who could answer that question—Sam Dixon. James really didn't want to call him. For all he knew, Sam was in on the whole thing. The man could be trying to lure him into a trap. The whole warning that the cult was after him could be nothing more than some elaborate plot to get rid of a witness.

Of course, there was such a thing as going into a trap with open eyes, knowing that your enemy didn't know you knew. He'd read that in a book once. It made sense. He waited until Maad had finished eating and left to throw away his Styrofoam tray before he dialed the number Sam gave him.

"This is Sam Dixon. I'm a little busy at the moment, but I'll get back to you in two shakes of a lamb's tail. Have a blessed day."

James scowled. When he actually wanted to talk to the man, he was nowhere to be found.

Then he took a second look at his phone. He was going to meet up with Amber. Part of him wondered if this would be a good excuse to stand her up. He didn't need to get involved with a girl, not now. Hell, this might even put her in danger. That's what happened in the movies. Villains were always taking the hero's wife or girlfriend hostage or murdering them out of spite and stuffing them in refrigerators. He didn't want that happening to Amber.

No. He'd said he'd meet up with her for ice cream and tell her what had happened. Maybe that'd be stupid, but he would keep his word.

Amber had expected Jessica and Ellen to be upset when they learned she was meeting up with James that afternoon. They didn't disappoint.

"You're going *out* with him?" Jessica demanded. Both her hands fell to the cafeteria table on either side of her lunch tray, the slap audible even over the noise of fifth-period lunch. "Amber, have you lost your mind?"

Amber's cheeks reddened. *If only that were true.* "We're not going out! And it's not like I'm getting in the car with him anyway. We're meeting at the Baskin and Robbins after school."

"That's better," Ellen said. "At least you can get out of there if he flips out. You want me to text you? It'll give you an excuse to leave, and if you don't answer..."

"That's sweet of you, but I don't think we'll be that long. He said he was going to tell me just what happened to Bill."

Silence fell for a long moment. Amber tensed. Had she said too much? If what she thought was going on actually was, James was in danger, she would be in danger if she were associated with him. Ellen and Jessica would be as well if the sons of bitches decided to be more thorough.

Jessica leaned forward. "Amber, you're tempting fate. Austin was a tool, but James could very well have *killed somebody* and avoided getting arrested because of..." Her lip curled in contempt. "Because of his daddy." She snorted. "Be patient. There're plenty of boys down at Valdosta who aren't murderers or just interested in one thing."

Amber rolled her eyes. "Jessica, it's not about that." It was about much, *much* more than that. "Anyway, if I wanted to date just anyone, I'd go out with *Walter*."

Jessica laughed, but it wasn't a kind one. Walter had tried to get her to go out with him too. "What time were you planning on meeting him?" Ellen asked.

Amber reflexively looked at her watch. "About 3:45. With traffic and all, it might take a bit to get out there."

"You know, Jessica and I could just 'happen' to show up there, maybe about fifteen minutes after you meet him," Ellen offered.

Amber sat up a little straighter. She couldn't fault her friends for trying to protect her from what they thought was a murderer. This wouldn't be the first time she'd made a poor decision as far as a boy was concerned. But if James told her what she suspected he was going to tell her, their lives might be in danger if they learned too much. She wouldn't do that. She *couldn't* do that.

Be cool. Don't freak out. Amber smiled. "Thank you for offering, Ellen. I don't think that'll be necessary." She looked at her watch. It was 1:15 in the afternoon. Classes ended at 3:30. "But if you two want to text me around 4:30, that'd be fine."

Ellen nodded. "That's fine with me. Jessica?"

Jessica pursed her lips. "I still think this is a bad idea, Amber. But I'm game."

———

THAT AFTERNOON after school let out, James made his way to the Baskin and Robbins as quickly as possible. Amber arrived barely five minutes after he did. Now she sat beside him in the front seat of his Saab in the parking lot. They'd both gotten cups of chocolate peanut-butter ice cream, but they'd long since stopped eating it.

James had started telling her the tale of the ATV race after they'd paid for their ice cream, but as soon as he got to the part about the water sloshing around, she immediately shushed him and hustled them out to his car. All she'd said was that they didn't know who might be listening.

"Okay," he said. "Why do you not want people talking about it? Is there some kind of death squad down here that kills everybody who talks?"

"Yes!" she exploded. She sighed. "Do you think they'd want word of what they're doing to get out?" She looked out the window. "Luckily you didn't say that much before I got you out of there." She looked straight at him. "What I'm about to say you *can't* repeat. Got it?"

"Sure."

Amber swallowed. "Dad told me that when he was little, his big brother was part of the cult. He'd joined it after fighting in Vietnam with one of them. Back in the Seventies, three civil rights workers from Atlanta came in, to register the blacks to vote. Only one left, and that was because my uncle hid him from the others. They found out." She swallowed. "They punished him."

"Punished him?"

She looked out the window again. "They took him to the tree farm. The thing in the woods ate him from the feet up. It took about an hour. Then the rest of them put on Klan robes and set his house on fire. Everybody figured he'd been an informer for the FBI, but that wasn't true at all."

The ice cream in James' stomach roiled uncomfortably. The hairs on the back of his neck rose. Bill's death had been horrific, but at least it had been quick. "The cult gave your uncle to...to the thing? Why didn't your family just get the hell out of here?"

Amber snorted. "Move? Run away? Let those bastards scare us off? This is our town too."

Her voice burned with long-buried anger. Time to change the subject. "How many people are in the cult?"

Amber shrugged. "Don't know, but I'd reckon it's smaller than it used to be. More folk are moving in and out of town these days, and that was before you all started showing up. But that doesn't mean it's not dangerous."

"I wasn't saying it's not." He paused. "Is Deputy Richards in it? Or Deputy Bowie?"

Amber sighed. "I don't know. I know what happened to my uncle because the man he met in Vietnam told Dad what really happened a couple years ago, when Dad was visiting people in the hospital with church."

A thought appeared in James' head, a thought that sent a wave of fearful tingling across his scalp. "Are any of your relatives in the cult?"

"No! Do you think they'd trust anyone from my family now? It's not that secret, especially those who've always lived here. But with more and more moving from Atlanta, odds're better and better someone who doesn't know not to talk is going to see something." Amber looked straight at him. "Guess who's the lucky man?" James' gut clenched. "Not only did you see it, but a whole bunch of folk know something happened involving you that led to a kid dying. A local kid. I don't know those deputies, but if they're not in the cult, maybe by blaming Bill for...what happened, they're trying to protect you as well as sweep the whole thing under the rug."

An attempted cover-up for his benefit? James had never thought of that. Deputy Bowie didn't seem like so much of a tool now. James frowned. He was still trying to cover up a murder enterprise. "Well, from what Sam told me, that little scheme doesn't seem to be working." He tensed. Why did he always realize he shouldn't have said something after he said it?

Amber's jaw dropped. "Sam? Sam Dixon?"

James hadn't been planning on telling Amber that, at least right away. But the cat was out of the bag now. He quickly relayed what Sam had told him after she'd left the Best Buy. "So how do you know Sam?" James asked when he was done.

"Sam's wife's dad was my mom's cousin, not sure to what degree. He died, and his wife remarried, but Brenda is still family." She paused. "It's complicated."

"Is everybody related to everybody down here?" He realized his mistake a moment after the words escaped his lips. *Shit.* That was twice in the same conversation.

Amber scowled. "Nobody here marries their cousins. But it *is* a close-knit community."

James nodded quickly. He must've hit a sore spot there. Best not keep jamming down on it. "You didn't know Sam was in the cult?"

She shook her head. "We're not that close. I mean, Sam and Brenda go to one of the Baptist churches on the West Side and we go to Creekside United Methodist."

James wondered just how divisive that could possibly be, but decided not to ask. He was running out of feet to stick in his mouth.

"Okay. Now what?"

"Well, the smart thing to do would be for your family to get the hell out of Edington. *Now.*" She looked out the window toward Fairmont Street and the acres of headstones in the cemetery beyond. "You and your other friends, especially Katie and Maad. *Especially* Katie and Maad." She paused. "On the other hand, that might be what they'll expect you all to do. They'll be watching the main roads in and out of the county."

James had a solution to that. His family's GPS had an option for back roads. If they had to get out of town by means other than the state highways, it wouldn't be that hard to figure a way out.

If they believed him of course. They'd thought he was on drugs when he told them what happened to Bill. If he told them this, with corroboration from Amber and Sam, they might be more willing to listen...

Suddenly his cheerful ringtone stabbed his ears. James snatched his phone from his jeans immediately. It was Mom.

"Shit!" James swore. Amber frowned. "Sorry. I'm grounded. For what happened with Bill." Amber gaped with outrage as James answered.

"Where are you?" Mom demanded before he could even say hello.

"I'm on the way to work," James said, hoping his lie was convincing. Well, it wasn't a *total* lie. He'd met up with Amber for ice cream after school. Then he'd be going to the Best Buy for his daily shift.

"Are you sure?" she asked. "I was driving by and saw what looked like your car parked in one of the strip malls. I thought it couldn't be you, but decided to check."

James' hand tightened on the phone. He hadn't thought about how that could happen. He'd forgotten that Mom would be coming home from the bookstore at some point in the afternoon. His gaze leaped to the long street ahead. He didn't see Mom's car anywhere. That didn't matter. The damage was done.

"One of Karen's friends wanted my help with school," James lied. "I figured I'd meet her on the way to work—"

"Is it that Amber girl?" James' heart skipped a beat. Amber's eyes bulged. Mom must've been so loud she heard her name over the phone. When Mom started talking again, she sounded both pissed off and amused. "After work, come straight home. You're grounded, remember? Your father and I are going to have to think of some additional punishment."

"Got it," James said, eager for the conversation to end.

"Goodbye."

"You're grounded?" Amber asked. "But you didn't do anything wrong! That's not fair at all!"

"You're telling me. Mom didn't like me being too argumentative, and Dad figured it'd keep me from hanging out with the people who were with me when…" He swallowed. "When Bill died. It might look like I was tampering with witnesses."

"All right," Amber said. "You tell your parents what's going on. I'll see if I can get hold of Sam."

CHAPTER TEN

Phillip and the employees working that day took advantage of the lull before the dinner crowd came to wipe down some tables. He was cleaning some spilled salt and pepper out from under their respective shakers when the door banged open. It was Sam. Phillip raised an eyebrow. The younger man looked upset.

"Phil," Sam began. His voice was louder than usual, his tone harsh. "Phil, you and me need to talk. Right now."

Phillip hadn't just fallen off the pumpkin truck. This had to be about congregation business. He looked around. Other than his employees, there were two customers present. None were congregants. Sam really should know better than to bring this up in public. He had to put a stop to this right now.

"I was wondering when you'd be coming by," Phillip said, just loudly enough to make a point. "I've got what you need in my office." He looked daggers at Sam. Hopefully that should get the point through his thick head.

Just like he hoped, Sam obediently followed him through the kitchen into the small room with frosted glass he used as his personal space. Phillip carefully closed the door before he let Sam have it. "What the hell is that about?" he demanded. "You come in here all riled, making a scene in my restaurant."

Sam swallowed. "It's about what happened the other night. You sent me and the rest to go kidnap a whole family over something one of their kids may have seen. And then when things go south, you feed Brother John to i...Him."

Phillip scowled. He'd reckoned sacrificing that fat idiot would only work in the short term. It'd take sacrificing the carpetbaggers to really fix the problem. However, he hadn't expected another challenge to his authority to come so soon, and he hadn't expected it from Sam. Things were worse than he'd thought.

"All four of you failed Him," Phillip explained in a tone appropriate for his grandchildren and Army pukes. "By rights, all four of you should have died. He showed mercy by only taking one."

"That's not the first time you've said something like that. But I'm not believing it this time."

"So? Standing in front of an oncoming car and claiming you don't believe in it doesn't mean you won't be squashed flat."

Sam didn't immediately answer. Phillip almost smiled. Perhaps that'd shut him up. He'd have to keep a closer eye on the younger man until this was done, of course, but that meant he didn't have to take more drastic measures. Sam was kin, sort of.

Then the younger man had to go and ruin it. "That's not the same thing, Phil. I don't care what kind of weird food they eat or whether or not they worship cows. That family didn't do anything wrong."

Phillip decided to take a different tack. "Sam, He works in mysterious ways. Maybe it was for the best." *If only I hadn't explicitly ordered the Indian family killed.* Then he *could* have claimed that He wanted to show Himself to them so that they would bring their kin into the congregation. It'd certainly help with the membership, however much Reed and those like him would piss and moan. Those who worshiped statues and cows would be easier recruits than those brought up thinking God was a spirit and not a physical being anyway.

"How's being *sacrificed* for the best?"

Phil's hand slid down toward his holstered pistol. He could shoot Sam now, take him by surprise. It wouldn't be that hard to claim he'd had come there with violent intentions, especially given how he'd challenged Phillip in front of his staff. The restaurant was in the unincorporated county, and there were congregants in the Sheriff's Office. Between that and Georgia's friendly attitude toward self-defense, that'd be it.

No. There were times where he'd been tempted to order his first sergeant to make some pissant draftee walk point so they'd step on a land mine or be the first to die in an ambush, but he'd never abused his power the way other platoon lieutenants had. And many of those who'd been whining, spoiled hippies Stateside had made fine Marines, eventually. Sam was getting troublesome, but this wasn't like passing dope around the camp or stirring up racial crap like some of the white trash did.

Phillip looked at his watch. The dinner crowd—such as it was these days—would start arriving in an hour or two. He really didn't have time for this bullshit right now.

"Sam, I've got work to do. How about we discuss this in more detail tonight?"

Sam looked at Phillip a bit too rebelliously for his taste. Phillip's hand slid closer to his gun. He'd make it quick, a shot to the head. A gut-shot would take a long time in killing and the odds Sam would survive once the ambulance was called were too great.

"All right," Sam conceded.

Phillip almost sighed in relief. "I'm glad you and I can see eye to eye."

Sam turned and walked out of the office. Once he saw Sam leaving the restaurant on the screen linked to the security cameras, Phillip reached over to his tan desk phone. He had some work for Reed.

Then something black on the screen caught his eye. His hand fell away. This was something he had to see to personally.

Phillip had almost stayed home that day. He had a couple episodes of *Lie To Me* recorded, and he hadn't taken a day off in over a week. He could relax, let his subordinates mind the store for him. And if he hadn't been there for Sam to argue with, the younger man might've expended his doubts all by his lonesome rather than had them validated by his actually acknowledging them.

But now, as the tall man in the dark suit and sunglasses approached the counter, Phillip was glad he'd saved Tim Roth's lessons on detecting body language for after the congregation's gathering that night. This one would probably claim to be some businessman passing through town, but Phillip had seen his kind before.

Three of them had come in from Atlanta just after he'd returned from Vietnam. He hadn't particularly cared if any of Edington's blacks voted or not—provided they didn't vote for Communists, overly-radical unions, or other disruptive elements—but most of the congregation and the high priest had, and he always followed orders. He'd led the congregation's strike team that killed two of the interlopers in that shitty motel they were staying in on the north side. They'd have gotten all three of them if it weren't for the damned traitor.

Phillip looked the man up and down. The stranger looked like an Atlanta businessman, or somebody from the

Chamber of Commerce who'd decided to dress up. But there were bulges under his arms an unwary man wouldn't notice. Phillip narrowed his eyes. This man clearly didn't believe in "non-violence" like his predecessors had. Phillip checked his hand's drift toward his own pistol and put on a big fake smile.

"How can I help you?" he asked. "It's a little early for dinner, but we've got plenty that can take the edge off."

The man didn't immediately respond. His head was angled slightly back, enough to take in the menu over the counter without taking his eyes off Phillip. For his part, Phillip didn't let his eyes leave the stranger either.

"I've always been partial to macaroni and cheese," the man said, in an accent Phillip couldn't quite place. *Damnation.* The three interlopers had sounded much the same.

Phillip nodded quickly. "Best macaroni and cheese in town. We use real butter." *Unlike that Kraft crap they serve across the street.* "It goes well with brisket."

"Sounds good. I'll have the smallest portion of each. Can't linger."

Phillip whistled to the cooks behind him and passed the man's order along. The man quickly paid for his meal, using small bills. Phillip checked the urge to frown. If the stranger used a credit card, that might provide a clue or two about his identity and purpose.

"It'll be a second until it's ready. What brings you to Edington?"

The man smiled, but the frown lines between the dark lenses concealing his eyes twitched. Phillip's grin widened, and it wasn't fake this time. The man had handed him the knowledge that whatever he was about to say wouldn't be true, or at least not entirely, on a silver platter. It looked like watching *Lie to Me* had paid off.

"I'm an insurance investigator. Somebody in town was in a car accident a couple days ago. I'm here to check it out."

The man was a much an insurance investigator as Phillip was an authentic, washed in the blood Baptist. No insurance investigator carried two guns in a shoulder holster, not unless they were operating in the hard ghettoes of Atlanta and probably not even then. And he was going out of his way to not only use cash—which could not be tracked electronically—but to use small bills that wouldn't draw attention.

That carpetbagger kid saw Him and escaped. He had to execute Thomas to maintain discipline in the congregation. Sam was wavering more than ever. And now this stranger shows up in Edington, a wolf in sheep's clothing. Fear began its slow creep up his spine. Sweat began beading under his gray hair. Phillip deliberately slowed his breathing down. He wouldn't show fear before this interloper.

"Sorry to hear about that." Phillip knew how the game was played. "Anybody hurt?"

"Nope. But I did hear something about a facial injury. And we can't find one of the people involved in the accident."

Facial injury. A missing man. That carpetbagger kid. John Thomas. The man in black knew some things he shouldn't. Either he was an inexperienced FBI agent—or Secret Serviceman or whatever the hell he was—unskilled in OpSec, or he was deliberately dropping hints in hopes of tricking a revealing reaction from Phillip. Sly bastard was probably trying the latter.

"Well, that's no good. I read the local paper every day, and I haven't heard anything about that."

"The local paper probably hasn't gotten the week's police reports. I imagine you'll hear about it soon enough."

Phillip kept up his friendly façade, but now anger warred with fear inside him. That last sentence had to be a threat. This

Atlanta bastard comes into his town, into his restaurant, and threatens him? He almost wanted the son of a bitch to come to the tree farm. Let the man in black see what happens when one challenges a god.

He looked away from the stranger before his anger broke out on his face. His attention fell on his employees. The plate brimming with blackened brisket and golden mac and cheese sat ready on the tray now. All that remained were the napkins and utensils.

"Looks like your food is ready, sir," he called out loud enough for the man to hear. He stepped forward to take the tray himself, leaving one of his cooks standing there with the napkin, fork, and knife in his hands. He set the tray on the counter in front of the interloper and then turned to take the napkin, knife, and fork from the cook. The younger man recoiled at the expression marring Phillip's face—good—but the high priest had his false smile back on by the time he turned back to the intruder with the utensils.

"Thanks," the man said. He took his food and retreated to a table by the door. But rather than set to it immediately, he removed what looked like one of those new iPhones from a belt clip and started typing something. Phillip's lips were a thin line. Typing something about *him* no doubt. After a few moments, the man put his phone away and finally started eating. Phillip watched him anyway. Phillip watched the man until he left the restaurant.

And once the enemy spy was gone, it was time for war.

————

BACK IN HIS OFFICE, Phillip went immediately back to his phone. The presence of this intruder changed everything. He didn't just need for Sam to be taught a lesson. No, Sam needed to be sidelined for the next few days at least. He couldn't have some loose cannon fucking things up while he made sure the stranger could never make contact with the carpetbagger kid.

Phillip dialed Reed's number, but it went straight to voicemail. Phillip almost smiled. Reed must be at work. With everybody tapping on their smartphones day and night, he could respect a willingness to put it aside and give one's all on the clock. He dialed the gas station.

"Hello?" a young voice he didn't recognize answered.

"My name is Phillip Davidson. I'm looking for Jeffrey Reed. Is he available?"

Silence. "He's stepped away for the moment. You want to call back?"

"How long do you think it'll be?"

"No more than two or three minutes."

"I can hold." Time passed. Phillip drummed his fingers on the desk. Sam might already be doing something stupid like trying to warn the carpetbagger kids or spread his rot among other congregants. If it got too far, he'd have no choice but to kill him. Even if he was a fellow vet and a kinsman besides.

"Brother Phillip?"

"Brother Jeffrey, can we speak privately?"

Phillip imagined a nod on the other side. "Yes sir." The line clicked off. A moment passed. Phillip's phone rang again.

"Hello?"

It wasn't Reed. "Hey Phil, it's Carlton. There's been some kind of accident on 285. The pork butt shipment's going to be late."

Damnation. He didn't need a business call right now.

"I understand," Phillip said quickly, letting only the slightest hint of irritation into his voice. "I've got an important call I need to take, so if that's it, don't worry about it."

"Thank you, sir." He put the phone back down on its cradle

a bit harder than necessary. Another moment passed. The phone rang again. If it was Carlton, no matter how cheerful that man was, he was going to find a new distributor. He didn't have time for this bullshit.

"It's Reed. I'm in the woods out back so nobody can hear me."

Reed wasn't a veteran far as Phillip knew, but he knew his OpSec. A pity Sam didn't, but he was an Army puke after all. "Good. I've got a job for you."

"One of those kids?" His old eagerness was there. Good. "I won't fuck up this time."

"Nope. It's Sam."

"Sam?" Reed sounded shocked. Phillip wasn't surprised. It had been decades since there'd been a purge. Congregant was not to harm congregant except at the command of the high priest. This was one of those times, but Phillip didn't expect Reed to know that.

"Yes, Sam. He's being insubordinate. You know how that's dealt with."

"Yes sir." Phillip imagined Reed grinning when he said that. When all one had was a hammer, everything looked like a nail. "You want me to kill him?"

Part of Phillip wondered if he should let Reed kill Sam. Someone with Sam's attitude was a liability, especially now that He had shed Edington blood and there was an outsider wolf in the fold. He had all confidence that the power in the woods that had protected the town and the faithful for centuries would triumph, but a member of the congregation going off the reservation could make things more difficult than necessary.

No. He'd sacrificed Tolliver because the man was an irredeemable drunk. Sam could still be salvaged. And there was

Brenda to worry about too. She didn't need to lose her baby *and* her husband.

"No. Just kick some sense into him. Tell him that he should have more faith. He'll understand."

"Yes sir." A pause. "Do you want me to do anything else?" There was eagerness in his voice. Maybe Reed still wanted to kill Sam or have some fun with Brenda.

Phillip's still-impressive muscles tensed at that unwelcome thought. If Reed laid a hand on Brenda, he'd die even more slowly than the traitor Phillip brought before Him decades ago. And with that attitude, he'd probably go overboard on Sam too. Phillip would need to be very specific.

"No. At the absolute most, I want him laid up for the next two days. No more damage to him that the minimal requirements for that, and no harm to *anybody else*. If you exceed my orders—and I will be the judge of that, not you—you will have Him to deal with. *Slowly*. Do I make myself clear?"

A pause. "Yes sir." He didn't sound so gleeful. Good.

"I'm glad we understand each other. This needs to be done today. I'm sure you can leave that kid running the gas station for an hour or so."

"He's a good kid. It won't be a problem."

"Excellent."

Phillip hung up, then started dialing the Sheriff's Office. They had to get that damn carpetbagger boy ASAP.

CHAPTER ELEVEN

"BRENDA?" SAM CALLED OUT AS HE STEPPED THROUGH THE front door. The screen door banged behind him. "Brenda, you home?"

Part of him hoped she wasn't. After the miscarriage three months ago, they'd both cried for a week. The heavy burden of sadness hadn't hung on him much longer, but it still weighed heavily on her. They'd been married since he got back from the Gulf, but try as they might they'd never managed a kid. Now there wasn't much time left. If she got out, that'd take that weight off her mind for a bit, cheer her up some. Sitting around the house didn't do a body any good at all.

Nobody answered. Sam looked through the doorway to the right, into the kitchen. The grocery list was missing from the refrigerator. Sam smiled. He'd been planning on getting that done himself, but she'd beaten him to the punch.

Then the screen door swung open with its characteristic screech. A chill ran up his spine. He'd forgotten to shut the main door. Footsteps squeaked on the linoleum. His Beretta was in the drawer by his bed. He'd thought to get a concealed-carry permit and keep it with him rather than where Brenda could get to it. But he'd never actually gone through with it.

And now somebody was in his house. Maybe it was just someone whose car had broken down, but they were pretty far from the main drag. He narrowed his eyes. He'd bet Phil sent somebody to shut him up. And there was one man in the congregation whom the high priest would turn to in a pinch.

"Why Brother Jeffrey." He didn't even turn around. "What brings you out here today?"

Reed snorted. "You're smarter than you let on. If you know it's me, you know why I'm here."

Reed had fifty pounds on him, most of it muscle. He'd have to be quick. Right for the throat. That was one of the kill-strikes he'd been trained to deliver if it came down to fists.

Sam feinted left before spinning right. Reed had moved left, but not as far as he needed to. He deflected Sam's throat chop with one hand and swung with the other. Sam dodged a blow that would have destroyed his ear.

Sam quickly retreated into the den and around the sofa, putting its threadbare green bulk between him and Reed. His gaze fell to the stone coasters on the coffee table. He'd left them out when he'd had friends over to watch the Braves game. He'd forgotten to pick them up, and Brenda hadn't done it either...

Sam had one in his fist as Reed came around the sofa. He swung for his enemy's chin. That should knock the big bastard out cold.

Reed kicked the coffee table straight into Sam's knees. Sam stumbled. His blow went wide. Reed's blow struck true, hitting Sam in the temple. His vision flashed black. He fell to his knees. A kick to the side laid him out.

"Phil says to have more faith in Him. I hope this will learn you a lesson."

He pulled back a booted foot for a kick that'd roll Sam into the brick fireplace. As the blow whistled in, Sam swatted it aside. Reed's foot passed over his hip. He kicked at Reed's leg, hoping he'd hit at just the right angle.

It worked. Reed toppled backward onto the couch. Its springs sang beneath his weight. Pain raging in the side of his head and just below his ribs, Sam pulled himself to his feet. He'd get the son of a bitch before he could rise. He leaped forward, landing knees-first in Reed's lap. He pulled back a fist, coaster still in hand, to put the man's lights out.

The screen door swung open again. Brenda slumped in, a brown bag of groceries from the nearby Piggly Wiggly in her slender hands. Her blue eyes widened as she took in the scene. The grocery bag fell from her hands, scattering food on the floor at her feet.

"Sam?" she asked. "Sam, what's—"

Reed took that as his moment to shove Sam onto the coffee table. The wood split beneath him, sending him crashing into the carpet below. Reed rose from the couch and glared behind him.

"You stay out of this if you know what's good for you!" he snarled. "I'm here on congregation business."

"Congregation business? Since when did *you* go to County Line?"

Sam took the opportunity to hit Reed in the back of the knee. The big man screamed. Maybe he'd just fucked up Reed's ACL.

"Get the Beretta!" Sam ordered. He'd feared what might happen if Brenda got her hands on it, but he'd worry about her mental state later.

Brenda's feet squeaked on the linoleum. Reed roared and lunged around the sofa, favoring his other leg. Sam grabbed him by the boot. He fell gut-first onto the floor. With luck that'd knock the wind out of him. Sam lunged, but Reed was faster.

He bounced back up and backhanded Sam, sending him stumbling across the living room.

"You get the hell away from my husband!" Brenda snarled. She stood in the hallway leading toward their bedroom. The pistol was raised, but it wasn't high enough. Sam hadn't gotten her lessons. Now he wished he had.

Reed charged. She raised the gun, but the big man grabbed it before she could level with his chest. The gun went off, an ear-splitting roar in the small room. Plaster sprayed from near the fireplace behind him. The bullet buried itself in the wall just beside the picture of their wedding day in Savannah, so long ago...

"Best give that gun to somebody who can use it," Reed growled. He struck her on the temple. Her curly brown hair whipped through the air as she slammed into the linoleum floor. Sam turned over, rage boiling inside him. He didn't care how much bigger Reed was or that he had the gun now. He'd shove that gun down his throat!

Reed loomed over him, the black pistol in hand. He shook his head. "I was just supposed to beat your ass so hard you'd be off your feet for a day or two. Just long enough to keep you from interfering. But you had to bring a gun into it. I'm not dumb enough to let you live, Phil or no Phil."

He brought up the Beretta, aiming straight at Sam's right eye. Sweat beaded on Sam's brow. That was a killing shot right there.

Then a brass lamp struck Reed on the side of the head. The big man staggered. He kept his arm straight, clearly trying to keep the gun on Sam, but ended up pointing the gun at the floral-painted wall.

Now or never.

Sam lunged, grabbing Reed's gun hand by the wrist. He

yanked the gun over his shoulder. Now all he had to worry about was another ricochet, but those could go anywhere.

Behind Reed stood Amber, still clutching the lamp tightly. Amber? What the hell was she doing here? School was out by now, but surely she had homework, or maybe that drama stuff she loved so much. He looked to Brenda. She was pulling herself onto her hands and knees, a huge bruise already blooming on her face.

Reed wasn't out of it yet. He spun Amber's way, murder in his eyes. Fortunately Amber didn't hesitate. Blood and teeth flew as her second blow shattered his face. He stumbled backward and fell onto the floor, his head bouncing off the fireplace.

Sam pulled himself to his feet. Reed lay there unmoving. Sam leaned forward. *He breathing?* There was one way to find out. He reared back and kicked Reed in the groin. The big man jerked but stayed out. Sam breathed in and out. "Thanks, Amber."

Amber looked around. "Does anyone know to shut the door around here? Jeez." She looked down at Reed. "Was he sent here to kill you?"

Sam shook his head. "Don't think so. Looks like he exceeded orders." He looked back at the fallen man. "Now what the hell am I supposed to do with him?"

"Tie him up, Sam," Brenda said, more vigor and firmness in her voice than had been there in months. "Hogtie him. With electrical cable. Then call the sheriff."

Sam frowned. If they called the Sheriff's Office, chances were Deputy Bowie would find out. He didn't need that, not at *all*. But it's not like they could just bundle him into the truck and take him to the Edington P.D. or the Highway Patrol, either.

He turned to Amber. "Thanks for showing up when you did. But what brings you out here?"

"James told me what's going on, about how you talked to him. I came to see you." Her gaze settled on Reed. Her lip curled. "It looks like I got here just in time."

Realization hit Sam like a lightning bolt. Phil had talked about going after the kids from Atlanta, but now he was going through with it. James was the only definite witness to Him. And Phil had sent Reed to get him out of the way. The high priest planned to feed even more innocents to the thing in the woods.

Well, Sam Garner Dixon was not going to allow that to happen. No sir. "Did you warn James?"

Amber nodded. "He was going to tell his parents."

"Do you know where he lives?"

"I gave his sister Karen a ride home the other day." Her face twisted with thought. "It's on the north side, beyond the city limits. It'll take a while to get there."

"You remember the way?" Amber nodded. "Good." If Phil was going after James, chances are he'd want to get the whole family at once. That meant he'd probably hit them around dinner-time. Sam looked at his watch. 5:15 p.m. He swallowed. If he wanted to join them, he wouldn't have much time.

Brenda was back on her feet now. "Sam?" she asked. "Sam, what's going on?"

Sam's throat clenched. He'd never told her he was part of the congregation. He'd assumed she'd known, being related to Phil, however distantly. He looked at her. Except for the bruise, she was white as a sheet, her eyes wide. She was already upset enough. He didn't want to burden her even more. But he couldn't lie to her neither. His mouth worked. Nothing came out.

He looked at his watch again. Time was a-wasting.

He didn't have any other choice. Phil would be after him as a traitor, and everybody in the congregation knew what happened to traitors. And if Reed didn't come back from his mission, retribution would come sooner rather than later.

Sam looked at Reed. Phil wouldn't expect his pet thug back for some time. If he were quick, he could get everybody out of this pickle.

CHAPTER TWELVE

Mom's shouting had begun as soon as James came in the door and hadn't let up since.

"With the scores you've made on those AP tests you have got to know what *grounded* means!" she snarled, pacing the hardwood kitchen floor in front of James. "That means when you're not at work or at school, you're at home. Not out socializing with your friends and certainly not out on a *date!*"

"It wasn't a date," James protested. It might've been nice if it were, but if it had been, it would have been the most morbid date ever. "She was telling me—" James' jaw clamped shut. How exactly was he going to tell his parents about a cult that had been worshiping a monster older than the United States? They hadn't questioned him too much about the thing that killed Bill, but maybe they'd hoped it would all go away.

Dad had been standing at the counter watching the spectacle. Now it was his turn to speak. "What was she telling you?" His voice was grave. He had to suspect something.

James swallowed. He wasn't going to be getting out of it

now. So he began with what happened to Maad and then the encounter with Amber at the Best Buy.

"Wait a minute," Dad interrupted. "One of the deputies has been talking about this? Spreading rumors all over town?"

James nodded. "She didn't say just *what* he said, but she wanted to make sure I hadn't killed Bill. She was awfully concerned about that."

Dad scowled. "When we're done with this, I'm going to have to call the Sheriff's Office. What those deputies have done is called poisoning a jury pool." He pulled his phone from his jeans pocket and began typing. "Now what?"

James got to Sam and the book he'd been told to read. He left out the part about Karen's blackmail. Although that might redirect some of Mom's fury, his heart wasn't in it.

"Hold on," Mom interrupted. "This man you don't know from Adam tells you there's this cult worshiping a monster in the woods and sends you to read some book that should be selling for fifty cents at my store 'proving' there's a monster in the woods. How do you know he didn't just put the book there himself? You start claiming the book proves you didn't kill that boy and suddenly the book's nowhere to be found. You'd look like a crazy person!"

"Andrea," Dad interrupted. "That's a stretch."

"Nobody had touched that book in years!" James protested. "He didn't put it there as part of some plan!"

"Well, I hope not. The way everybody's related around here, I wouldn't put it past them—"

"Is there more to the story?" Dad interrupted.

So James finished, ending with the talk with Amber in the car. "That's two different people. Do you think I'm crazy now?"

Dad's lips were a thin line. "That certainly changes some things."

"They're family though," Mom said. "Maybe she's trying to set you up too."

James shook his head. "No Mom, no she wouldn't. She's—" James shut up again. Amber was smart. Amber was spirited. Despite the circumstances, he'd liked spending the time with her he had. But did he really want to tell Mom this? He could feel his cheeks turning red.

"Look, I know she's friends with Karen. And Karen will be positively tickled if you two start going out." James rolled his eyes. "But the timing is a bit suspicious, don't you think?"

"Andrea," Dad interrupted. "James, go to your room. Your mother and I will discuss this further. We'll call you down if we need you."

James was glad to get out of the conversation without any more punishments. He quickly retreated upstairs. He flopped down on the bed and stared at the cream-colored ceiling.

Mom was right. This was insane. Immortal monsters worshiped in the woods? Cults secretly killing people for hundreds of years? What were the odds? Maybe Amber and Sam were playing some kind of prank on him. There was more than one way to screw with a "carpetbagger" than by challenging him to a race. Luckily, he'd managed to find someone to work his shift at Best Buy that afternoon so their plan wouldn't cost him his job...

He shook his head. Even if they were in cahoots for some reason, that didn't mean what happened that afternoon in the woods was a figment of his imagination. *Something* had come out of the water. *Something* had killed Bill in front of him. His hand wandered to his bandaged cheek. *Something* had split open his face like a butcher's cleaver.

He continued staring up at the ceiling. Things started to blur. Then the sudden ringing of his phone jolted him alert. He snatched it up. Was it Amber? No, it couldn't be. They'd never actually exchanged numbers.

It was Sam. What did he want? James nearly answered it. But he didn't. The day had been difficult enough. He didn't need any more drama.

Eventually, the phone stopped ringing. Soon afterward came two buzzes. Voice mail. He'd get to that, but not right now. He lay back and looked up at the ceiling, its smooth uniformity broken only by the vent over his bed.

Smooth like the black flesh of the monster. Cream-colored just like the multitude of teeth. The grille of the vent opening like a mouth...

Checking his voice-mail seemed a lot more interesting right then. The family phone plan still included transcribing voice-mails to text. He didn't even need to bring the phone to his ear or listen to anybody talking in real time.

What came next made his gut clench.

The congregation is moving. They're going to your house. You and yours, get the hell out of there. Now!

James jumped to his feet. That got him a glimpse out the window.

Deputy Bowie was coming out of the woods. Behind him, hard to see against the green and brown of the trees, were men in camouflage. *Armed* men.

The cultists were already there.

———

BY THE TIME James got downstairs, they were already in the house. Sounds of men shouting and dishes crashing came from the kitchen. He got a brief glimpse of Bowie with his knee in Dad's back cuffing his father's hands behind him. The others had followed the deputy inside, but luckily he was able to retreat into the hall closet before anyone noticed him.

Part of him wanted to call the police immediately. Handling home invasions was their job. That's what he'd always been taught. But every time his thumb reached for the digit 9, he remembered that one of the people ransacking his house was a cop. He'd have to wait this one out. But there were a whole bunch of cultists. How long would it take them to find his hiding place? It shouldn't take long at all, not unless they were complete idiots. Something shattered outside. They were hunting him.

James' phone buzzed in his pocket. Though nobody should be able to hear it, his heart leaped into his throat. Should he answer it? He couldn't answer it. Any movement, let alone any words, would alert the rednecks tramping through his house that somebody was hiding in the closet.

The phone buzzed again. James shook his head. He wasn't going to risk it. Wait for the bastards to leave, then call the cops. Even if half the local police were in the cult—and from what Amber said it probably wasn't that many—the odds of survival were better than if he let himself fall into the cultists' bloody hands. Something else smashed outside, closer this time.

Seconds passed in the darkness. The phone buzzed twice. James slipped the phone out of his pocket. It was Sam.

The congregation is at your house. Answer your phone. I can help you.

James shook his head. Sam had "warned" him and then these rednecks showed up. Either this was all a trick on Sam's part or the older man was simply an idiot. Either option left James hiding in the closet.

Boots tramped on the hardwood floor outside. James froze. The closet was a pitifully obvious hiding place. They'd tear the door open and drag him out. They'd take him to the woods, to face the thing. The wet smell of the woods and the iron smell of blood rushed back as he remembered Bill's death, his panicked flight from the creature with too many eyes and tentacles.

He suddenly needed to piss. He tensed, keeping even a single drop from leaking out. He wasn't going to wet himself again.

Bright light exploded into James' vision. When the sparks cleared from his eyes, he saw Sam standing there. The man looked pissed off. A handgun hung heavily from his hip.

"You really thought you could hide there? I reckoned someone who could get away from Him would be cleverer."

James leaped at Sam before the older man could move. His only chance was to knock Sam down, get the gun. Their combined weight slammed them into the opposite wall. James grabbed the gun. He tore at the scaly metal of the grip, but it wouldn't come free. Sam's rough hand seized his wrist. James rammed his knee into Sam's groin. That'd loosen his grip.

Sam turned both his knees inward, catching James' kneecap between his thighs. Slowly he forced James' hand away from the gun.

More footsteps, this time to the right. James' head snapped sideways. Another cultist, shorter than Sam and with a chipped front tooth, stood in the kitchen doorway. He carried a pistol in his right hand, although fortunately it was pointed downward. "Sam!" A syrupy accent, the thickest James had ever heard in Edington. "I didn't know you were coming on this hunt, but you've made quite an entrance."

"Yeah." Sam smiled. "I didn't want to disappoint Him today."

James tried to jerk away. He had to run. Sam's grip on his wrist was like an iron manacle, but he'd broken it before. He yanked with all his might. Sam wordlessly slammed his hand into the wall. He yelped.

"Where are the others?" Sam asked.

"The mother ran. No sign of the sister. No great loss." *Thank God.* At least Mom and Karen got away from the redneck bastards. "By the time they get help, we'll be long gone." He shrugged. "This is S.O. territory anyway. Even if either of them does get 'help,' they might end up with a one-way ticket to Him. Brother Charles got his pa." He grinned at James. "Think of it as a father-son sort of thing. He's trussed up nice and tight in my car." He looked to Sam. "Bring him there."

Sam shook his head. "Putting them both in one place means they can help each other escape. You bring the father. I'll bring the son."

A moment passed before the other cultist shrugged. "Works for me. I think I'll help myself to some of the furnishings around here." He smiled at James. "You got a nice house, kid."

He disappeared back into the kitchen. Sam turned to James. "C'mon. We can't keep Him waiting."

The thought of facing the monster in the trees was too much. James finally broke Sam's grip. He ran. The back door into the yard was still open. If he could get out in the woods, maybe he could lose them-

A booted foot caught him in the seat of his pants. He flew forward, the living room rug kinder to his elbows and forehead than the hardwood floor or the brick fireplace would have been. Before he could get up, a foot on the small of his back forced him back down.

The other cultist emerged from the kitchen, Mom's Cutco knife set under one arm. "You sure you got this?" Disdain was written on his ugly face. "He's a slippery little bastard."

"I got this," Sam said. Metal hissed free from leather. "If he tries to run again, I'll kneecap him." The boot vanished. "Get up."

The other cultist shrugged. "That's between you and Him."

Keeping his gun jammed into James' spine, Sam marched him out the front door. There was no police car. There was one car parked out front. Was that where they had Dad? James strained to look, but Sam forced him past it.

James kept his mouth shut as Sam forced him down the cul-de-sac. Trees crept from the woods between the houses. In front of one of the empty houses sat a red truck. There was someone sitting in the front seat. As they got closer, horror bloomed in James' chest. The redneck son of a bitch had Amber!

James' eyes bulged. The bastards were going to kill Dad, they were going to kill him, and they were going to kill her too!

James lunged for the truck, not caring that Sam had a gun. He'd get in the truck, get Amber away from this redneck cultist and—

Sam hit him hard between the shoulders, knocking him onto his knees. The black asphalt, cracked from lack of maintenance, bit his hands. But James didn't fall on his face like he'd done in the house. Instead, he twisted his body and swung. His fist caught Sam's wrist. The gun clattered on the pavement. It didn't go off.

Sam grabbed for the gun, but James was closer. He snatched up the weapon and scrambled back against the warm metal of the hood. Nowhere to run now. He pointed the gun straight at Sam's chest, remembering things those more interested in firearms had said about aiming for the center of mass.

Now he had the treacherous bastard at his mercy. He'd find out where they were taking Dad and then he'd blow the redneck's brains out. The cult would have no warning he was coming for them.

The passenger door of Sam's truck clanged open beside him. "James, wait!" Amber hissed. "He's not one of them!"

"Yes he is," James snarled, still pointing the gun at Sam. He kept his eyes locked on those of his enemy. If he looked away even for a second, Sam would rush him. They weren't that far apart.

"No!" Amber stepped between James and Sam. "This is all a setup. He's going to help us rescue your Dad and put an end to the cult for good." Amber pointed to the house, still somewhat visible through the trees. "If they don't see you with the gun on him, of course."

"Get in the truck," Sam ordered. "Both of you. We'll discuss it there, where they can't see us."

"Listen to him," Amber implored. "You trust me, right?"

Maybe he did, maybe he didn't. Amber was smart and pretty. James enjoyed her company, surprisingly enough. But she *was* related to Sam, however distantly. Maybe the story about the cult killing her uncle was made up, or maybe she wanted to buy her way back into their good graces with his life.

Amber looked at him, soft eyes wide. "Please, James."

James lowered the gun. "All right. But I'm keeping this." He kept his eyes on Sam. "You try anything, even once and—"

"You ever killed a man?" Sam growled. James didn't immediately answer. "I have, at the Battle of Medina Ridge in the first war with Iraq. That was before you were even born. That means where war is concerned, I'm in charge. Get in the damn truck."

James peered over Sam's shoulder back at the house. The cultists were coming out the front door, including the ugly bastard now carrying the knife set under one arm and Dad's old portable CD player under the other. They'd see what was going on. He didn't know how many bullets this gun had, but surely it'd be enough to kill five people.

"James!" Amber hissed.

The people were walking down James' yard to the car

where they'd stashed Dad. It looked like there were only three. The rest must've returned to the woods.

"All right." Amber quickly had the door open and the two scrambled inside. Sam brought up the rear as James squeezed himself into the narrow seat behind the driver. If Sam tried anything, he'd blow his brains out all over the dashboard.

CHAPTER THIRTEEN

Before James could react, Sam snatched the gun from his hands. He clicked a button on the side—must be the safety—and jammed it barrel-down into the black cup holder between his and Amber's seats.

"I've got weapons for you at the house," Sam declared. "But not this one." Then the anger flowed away from Sam's face, replaced by his previous amiability. "I'm sorry. I had to look like a loyal congregant to get you out of there."

That didn't make the pain from the various small injuries Sam had inflicted or the annoyance he'd snatched the gun back at first opportunity go away. "Fine." He watched Sam as they pulled onto the road that led to Fayetteville Boulevard. "What the hell is going on here?"

"I gave Phil a piece of my mind," Sam said. "And he sent his bullyboy Reed to my house. If Amber here hadn't showed up, I don't know what that piece of shit—begging your pardon— would have done." He fell silent for a moment. "He wants to kill you and all your friends, anybody who might have seen it that afternoon. And he's right pissed. He offered up a loyal congregant the other night. If he can't get you, I imagine he'll kill your pa."

"Wait a second. Who's Phil?"

"The leader of the congregation," Amber said. "He owns the barbecue joint through the woods there." She pointed toward the trees lining the southbound side of Fayetteville Boulevard. James' gaze followed. Across from the corpse of what used to be a sushi restaurant and just before the first big strip mall flashed red brick and brown wood and a pickup truck's bright blue. He swallowed. The evil mastermind was *that* close?

James' hand crept toward the gun in the cup holder. He checked the movement. Now was *not* the time to get into another fight over that gun. "So what now?"

"My wife is calling the Edington cops." Sam turned left onto the main drag. "The congregation has only one or two members there, and they're low-ranked. But by the time they get out to the tree farm, your pa'll be dead."

James' gut clenched. He remembered the thing rising out of the water, Bill impaled on the claws at the end of its tentacles. Blood pouring out of his mouth... He shook his head, driving the images away. That couldn't happen to Dad. He wouldn't let it.

"That's where we come in," Amber said. "We're going to rescue him."

That sounded like fun. These animals were murdering people, feeding them to a monster, and they'd been doing it for hundreds of years. They deserved to die, all of them, and he'd gladly be the one to do it.

Then a bucket of ice water crashed across his angry thoughts. "There are three of us. Three of us against a bunch of cultists and..." He swallowed. "*It*. What the hell are we supposed to do?"

THE THING IN THE WOODS   141

"Nobody but Phil and Reed have any reason to not trust me, and Brenda has Reed under control. Both of you'll get in the back of my truck, under a tarp, and I'll get the three of us to the sanctuary." He paused. "The place of sacrifice."

Place of sacrifice. James didn't like the sound of that one bit.

The truck crossed Fairmont and turned off past a Burger King. It wasn't long until they pulled into a neighborhood of neat, white-painted single-story houses. They were a little small for James' taste. One house had an old Accord sitting in the driveway. Sam pulled the truck in beside it. When the doors opened, Sam and Amber spilled out. James had to move quickly to catch up. He still kept an eye on Sam and, more importantly, the gun. Best be careful.

The first thing James saw when they got inside was a big man hogtied on his side by the fireplace, beside a tiny brown-haired woman who watched him with her grip tight on a butcher knife. Dried blood caked his face around his badly broken nose. "That Reed?"

Sam nodded. "Amber put him out."

James looked at Amber. He raised an eyebrow. "You did that?"

Amber nodded. "Brass lamps can do a lot of damage when you hit someone a bunch of times in the head."

James laughed. He hadn't expected that from Amber. "Good job."

The woman rose from the fireplace. She rushed over to Sam. "He's been out the whole time. I called the police, but they haven't come."

James' jaw nearly dropped. It had to have been half an hour at least since he'd gotten the text. He'd heard of slow response times, but Sam's house was close to Fairmont Street. What the hell was going on?

"There're congregants in the police department. Not many, but maybe they're in a position to sit on the call. We'll definitely have to hit the tree farm now, if they're delayed."

"Congregants?" the woman asked. "I don't know anyone from church who's in the Police Department."

"Honey, not our church," Sam said. "Something else."

Realization danced across the woman's face. "You mean...?"

Sam nodded gravely. Her jaw dropped. Anger crossed her features.

Oh boy. Here it comes...

"Sam, really? After all we've been through, now *this*?"

The woman sank back down onto the fireplace.

"Brenda, I know this is all a lot to take in. But not now. They went after the boy but only got his pa. Chances are they're going to kill him instead. Feed him to a *monster*."

James watched the conversation. Sam's wife didn't know what he was up to and this was how she found out? Assuming they came back alive, Sam would be sleeping on the couch for the next year or two at least.

Sam turned back to James. "You've been to the outskirts of the tree farm, but never inside. As you get closer to where it lurks, the ground gets wetter. You'll need boots. Lucky you I've got two pairs."

He stepped down a hallway and returned with two pairs of Army boots. He handed one set to James and knelt down to untie his own shoes.

"Wait a minute," Amber interrupted. "I don't get boots?"

Sam looked up at her as he pulled off his sneakers and put on the boots. "You're going to guard the truck, in case anybody gets suspicious."

Amber scowled but said nothing as Sam finished lacing on his boots. It took James a bit longer to get them on properly. When he rose to his feet, Sam gestured for him and Amber to follow him down the hall. The trio passed through the small bedroom into a smaller closet. At the back of the closet, beyond the hanging clothes, stood a big brown safe with a silver circular lock.

"We'll need more than my Beretta to take on the congregation. And Brenda'll need that if Reed ever wakes up."

Sam twirled the combination lock on the gun safe. Before that afternoon, James hadn't handled a gun in years, not since he dropped out of the Boy Scouts sophomore year. Did Sam expect him to actually shoot it and hit what he was shooting at? Sweat beaded on his brow. Hit *people*? He'd had the gun on Sam, but he was pissed then. He'd have to kill men in cold blood now. This wasn't paintball.

The safe popped open. Inside were a long rifle and a matched pair of shotguns with long tubes under the barrels. At the bottom were some curving plastic things half-buried in magazines of various types. Sam reached down and picked out two magazines that didn't curve. "How much shooting do you do?"

James swallowed. "None in real life, not in years. Something tells me playing *Call of Duty* or *HALO* doesn't count."

Sam shook his head. "No sir it doesn't. You'll get the shotgun. You won't need to be as accurate."

That was *somewhat* better. He'd at least shot skeet before. He knew how to eject the shells and reload. Sam handed James the shotgun and a box of shells. James kept the weapon pointed straight up. He didn't want to shoot off his own foot by mistake. Sam picked up one of the plastic devices from the bottom of the safe. It was then that James saw the marking "Front Toward Enemy."

"Holy shit. Are those *Claymores*?" He'd seen pictures of them, but never one in the lethal plastic and ball-bearing flesh.

Sam nodded. "Yep. I've got some friends at the National

Guard armory a couple streets over."

"Friends who gave you *Claymore mines*?"

Sam sighed. "Loaned me the Claymore mines. Just in case. If I didn't need them, I'd give them back. They do inspect what they've got, you know, sometimes without announcing it. One of those can turn most of the congregation to jelly if we have to. The other's in case *He* shows up. Third's a spare."

James frowned. Did Sam detour on the way to his house to get those mines and then drive back? If he hadn't done that, could he have gotten there earlier and kept the whole mess from happening?

Before James could ask, Sam set the Claymore down on the hardwood floor and took the rifle out of the safe. "You know what this is?"

James looked at it. "An M-16?" Were those even legal?

Sam shook his head. "AR-15. Close enough. An M-16 can fire full-auto." He shook his head. "Never had much use for that myself. There're better weapons for suppressing fire. But suppressing fire is what we'll need today, so I'll just keep pumping that trigger."

Suppressing fire. Keep enemy heads down. Hopefully in the path of the Claymore explosion. "That's the plan if the mine's not enough. You lay down the suppressing fire and..."

"And you run in and untie your pa." He hefted the second shotgun. "This's for you, Amber." He handed her the weapon. "God willing you won't actually need it, but if you do, don't hesitate one single second."

Amber swallowed. "Got it."

James looked at the gun safe. "I think we'll need more guns. Once we rescue Dad, he'll be able to shoot too and—"

"He ever shot? Recently?"

"I don't know!"

"If he hasn't, he's a danger to himself and others." He

looked at the two teens. "Putting guns in your hands is tricky enough, but I can't take them on all by my lonesome."

He headed for the door. Only God knew what horrible shit those redneck cultists were doing to Dad—

"Wait." Sam's words stopped him in his tracks.

"What?" His head snapped Sam's way. "We can't wait! Every minute we wait, the more likely it is my Dad's going to get fucking *sacrificed!*" He glared at Sam. "What do you *do* anyway? Rip out hearts, like in *Indiana Jones*, or maybe—"

"We need to pray," Sam declared simply.

"Pray?" James didn't want to disrespect someone else's religion, but they really didn't have time. And who was Sam going to pray to? The thing in the woods? The monstrosity that those cultists were going to sacrifice Dad to?

"Yes, pray." Sam bowed his head and set the AR-15 on the ground. Then he raised his hands like some holy roller. Amber bowed her head. James sighed and bowed his head as well. Hopefully this'd be over quickly.

"I've gone to County Line since I came back from the Gulf, but I'd also worshiped an abomination in the woods," Sam began. "It's written to have no other gods before the Lord and not to serve two masters." He paused. "Choose this day whom you will serve."

James raised an eyebrow. The Ten Commandments weren't hard to remember, but the other verses he quoted were more obscure. Despite himself, he was impressed.

"This day, I'm choosing who I'm going to serve," Sam continued. "I'm going to serve the real Lord."

"Amen," Brenda said from behind them. James let his gaze drift toward her. What was she going to do in all this mess? Just stay home with a tied-up thug waiting for the police to come get him while her husband took two kids to war?

Sam lowered his hands. "All right. Let's go."

CHAPTER FOURTEEN

JAMES AND AMBER LAY IN THE BACK OF SAM'S RED PICKUP truck between two heaps of firewood covered by a blue plastic tarp. It was warm, but not uncomfortably so. Not yet at least.

The truck rumbled over gravel to a stop. James gripped his shotgun so tightly his hands started to hurt. They must be at the entrance to the tree farm now. There wasn't much light under the tarp. The near-darkness made everything worse.

He swallowed. If they caught him, he was dead, and so were Sam and Amber. It wouldn't be a clean death. The thing the locals worshiped in the woods liked its meat living. And the cultists would probably want to have fun with Amber first.

He looked over at Amber. He wasn't going to let that happen. Not ever.

She reached over and took his hand. He gave her a squeeze. She smiled.

Feet tramped in the gravel outside. They both froze. James tried not to even breathe. If the cultists found them, he'd have to shoot them before they could react or he and Amber would both die. He swallowed. But then the cultists would know they had company. And Dad would die.

James thought back to when things were better. He and Dad had earned their SCUBA licenses together back when he was in middle school. They'd had their checkout dive at Destin, where the water was so clear one could see hundreds of feet all around. And Dad had hosted meetings of his Cub Scout pack and gone with him to Boy Scout summer camp, even that time it rained for most of the week.

Tears sprang to his eyes. He squeezed them shut. He wasn't going to cry in front of Amber and he sure as hell wasn't going to alert the cultists outside.

"You're late," someone growled beside the truck. "They're going to offer up that damn city-slicker lawyer soon. You'll get a poor seat for that."

"My own fault," Sam replied. "Brother Phillip sent me to help Brother Jeffrey in case he needed it catching that damn kid."

The smile Sam's clever lie brought to James' face quickly blew away. The best lie was the one that was mostly true, but if the cultist who'd seen Sam kidnap James happened to be around, they'd be exposed right away. He closed his eyes. He didn't want to be here. He didn't want to kill anybody. But he'd kill any number of these bastards to save Dad.

"Did Brother Jeffrey get the kid?" the man outside demanded. "My kid goes to school with him. Arrogant bastard won't mix with the kids from around here. Hangs out only with those Atlanta folk. Thinks we're all a bunch of dumb hicks."

This reddened James' face. He didn't know Amber all that well, but she wasn't some dumb hick. And even Bill, who he was pretty sure was, hadn't wanted him eaten. Who was the man talking about? He couldn't remember any of the locals who'd wanted to hang out with him and his friends. Had he ever given anyone the cold shoulder?

"I reckon he did, Brother Tyler. At least that's what he said on the phone. They do live out in the country a ways, so it might be a bit before they get here."

"Not too soon I hope. I want the little shit to see his father die before he goes into His mouth."

James scowled. Even if he had pushed away some local kid who wanted to befriend him, that man's attitude was overkill. Hopefully he'd get a chance to put a shell into his face by the time everything was said and done today.

"All in His timing, Brother Tyler, all in His timing."

A long moment passed. A bead of sweat trickled down James' side. Were Sam and this jackass Tyler whispering with each other? His ears perked. Try as he might, he couldn't hear anything. He couldn't move to get a better listen. Maybe Mom was right. Maybe the whole thing was a trap. And everything, including Sam's gaudy Baptist prayer, was a charade to get him to let his guard down.

Then the truck jolted forward. A huge weight lifted off James' chest. Whoever guarded the tree farm clearly hadn't been suspicious of James' cargo. Maybe they'd never had to deal with a suicide bomber. It'd be nice if someone went al-Qaeda on the cult and blew them all into chunky salsa, so long as it wasn't him.

The gravel under the truck grew rougher. The rumbling loosened the tarp. Light spilled into his and Amber's hiding place. When James finished blinking the stars from his vision, he saw Amber looking at him oddly.

"What?"

She laughed. "I like your freckles." She paused. Even in the shadows, James could see her blush. "You know, I've always wanted to count them."

James raised an eyebrow. "You're counting my freckles?"

"Yep." She reached out and touched the spray of freckles under his right eye with a warm finger. "Always wanted to. I think there's a least twenty right here. I wonder how many are on the other side?"

"I haven't done that since I was five. I think I lost count around one hundred." He swallowed. "I've got a bunch on my shoulders too." Maybe she'd get the chance to count those too. Now *that* would be fun. But not now.

The truck sped up. James was torn. The faster they got to the place of sacrifice, the better the odds Dad was still alive. But the faster they got there, the sooner they'd confront the monstrosity again. The image of the thing in the woods tearing away the sheltering tarp above them filled his mind. It'd look over them, its azure eyes spewing their morbid light. Its tentacles would fall like lightning, skewering them like spitted hot dogs at a cookout. It would lift them up in the air, blood dripping down on the truck like rain, before tossing them both into its huge mouth. *Alive* into its huge mouth.

His hands flashed to the tarp covering them. If the thing was coming, he wanted to see it rather than have it creep up on him.

"James!" Amber hissed. "What are you doing?"

The blue tarp spilled away as James sat up. He squinted against the light even brighter than the sliver that illuminated them a few minutes ago. But he could still see.

The fence surrounding the tree farm lay well behind, a thin gray streak through trees lined up as neatly as rows of corn. The underbrush had been cleared away, leaving long avenues paved with pine straw. The sun smiled through gaps in the canopy. It was warm, warmer than it had been when he'd last entered the domain of the thing in the woods.

The image of Bill rising in the air, crucified on the

monster's limbs rose from James' memories like an evil submarine. Sweat suddenly beaded on his forehead. His stomach surged into his mouth. He swallowed down the stinging bile, but his fear didn't go with it. They were going right into its lair, to the place the cultists had been feeding it living men for God knows how many hundreds of years. He was going to face it again. He suddenly had to piss.

No. Not this time.

Amber sat up beside him. She looked around. "Oh thank God." She looked over at him, anger clear on her face. "That could've been real bad if somebody saw us."

She had a point there.

"You ever been in here?" He pointed to the rows of trees. "I've never been to a tree farm before." He swallowed. "It actually looks kind of nice."

Amber shook her head. "There's plenty of real woods around here. East of Griffin there's High Falls State Park. My family and I went camping there last year. There's a great big lake. Beautiful waterfalls."

Despite the situation, James grew curious. "I've never been out there. I've been to Piedmont Park in Atlanta though. Freedom Park too." He swallowed. The two of them were about to go into the jaws of hell. Why was he going to ask now? This was not even a remotely appropriate time.

On the other hand, it wasn't like he really had anything to lose.

"How about this? Once we're done here"—he left the alternative unsaid—"We go to each other's favorite park? I show you Piedmont Park, you show me High Falls."

Amber grinned. "Why James Daly, are you asking me out?"

Now it was his turn to blush. "Sure."

Amber laughed. "I'd love to."

James felt strangely relieved. However, the bright spot in

the darkness was soon snuffed out when the truck jolted. His head whipped around. Had the thing come out of the water? He'd seen video of octopuses crawling onto land on YouTube. He could just imagine the freight train of glistening black flesh and too many eyes surging through the trees, its vast mouth opening wide to swallow him and Amber alive.

But nothing was coming. Sam must've hit a bump in the road. James reddened. Son of a bitch. At this rate, he'd stroke out before he ever saw a cultist, let alone the monster. And he'd look like a coward in front of Amber.

As they rolled deeper into the tree farm, things changed. The orderly rows gave way to the wild. Underbrush clawed at the flanks of the trees, their tendrils digging into the wooden flesh between the scaly bark. The canopy closed overhead. The temperature dropped. The ground grew wet.

James remembered the story of the Union soldiers chasing the Edington Home Guard—the cult by another name—into the "wet wood." There most of the men from Missouri had died, with the survivors not living much longer.

He looked down at the box at his feet. The Claymores made the cannons those soldiers probably didn't have look like Super Soakers. And unlike those poor men, the three riding into the wooded hell knew what they faced.

"Your gun loaded?" Whatever happened to him, he wanted Amber to be able to protect herself.

She nodded. "I've hunted before. Got a couple turkeys down by the reservoir."

"Good." If she could kill animals, maybe she could kill *people*.

Something glinted to James' left, through a gap in the wild trees. His head snapped to the side. It was a pond, opening like an enormous dark eye out of the wet ground. A pond just like the one the thing erupted from to attack Bill. He suddenly had to piss again. His grip on Amber's hand tightened.

The truck turned sharply around a bend, rolling Amber halfway on top of him. Under different circumstances he'd have liked that, but not now. "You all right?" Amber nodded. She didn't immediately pull away. That was cool. Part of him wanted to slip an arm around her and pull her closer. He might not get another chance.

Oh, what the hell.

Amber's eyes widened, but it was amusement and not distress that crossed her face. "Isn't this a little soon?"

His hand crept up her spine. "Not really."

She laughed and leaned in, her brow touching his. "I like that answer."

Unfortunately, there wasn't time for much more. Another turn and the trees pulled away from the road. James pulled himself up as much as he could without disrupting Amber to look over the rim of the truck bed. Ahead lay a bunch of cars, one of which had been in front of James' house earlier. A couple bore the blue and white of the Sheriff's Office. James' heart sank. Assuming two or three per car, there could be close to forty cultists present. The three of them couldn't possibly take them all on.

Then he saw what lay on the other side of the parking lot.

Beyond the cars, flanking a dirt path disappearing into the trees, stood two enormous carvings. They rose up twenty feet each and reminded James of Indian totem poles he'd seen on a family trip to the Field Museum in Chicago. They towered overhead like the poles in the Hall of Native North Americans, but there the resemblance ended. These weren't red cedar but some darker wood, as black as obsidian and just as shiny. Carved tentacles rippled up the pole until about two feet from the top. There, crowned with too many azure eyes, were hideous elongated heads with teeth, bright white and razor-sharp.

Fear surged through James. The hairs on the back of his neck rose at attention. His scalp tingled. He pointed. "You see that?"

Amber nodded. Her blue eyes locked on the two totem poles. Her grip on James' hand tightened. It was starting to hurt. She pressed harder against him. That at least wasn't so bad.

The truck pulled to a stop well off to the side, far from the other cars. *Harder to box in. Good call.* The engine cut off. A moment later, the door clanged open. Amber pulled away from James, but not before Sam came around. He looked at Amber, then at James. A ghost of a smile crossed his face before he pointed at the totem poles.

"Those were there when the first white men came." James frowned. There was an unsettling amount of awe in Sam's voice. "These're older than the Creeks. Maybe even older than the mound-builders. I'm not even sure men made them."

Now that was a little hard to swallow. Some redneck cult offering people they didn't like as human sacrifices, sure. Something that actually accepted these sacrifices, well, that was something he'd seen with his own eyes. But Marvin the Martian? He hoped there wasn't a grain of truth to that. He didn't want to get anal-probed on top of everything else.

"All right," Sam ordered. "Everybody out."

Both gripping their shotguns, James and Amber scrambled over the side of the truck bed. The gravel crunched loudly beneath their shoes. James' head snapped toward the path. Though the sound had thundered in his ears, nobody came to investigate. *Good.*

"Stay here," Sam ordered Amber before she could step away from the truck. He tossed her the keys. "Use the shotgun to protect yourself, but don't stir up trouble. If you have to, drive away and leave us."

Amber shook her head. "No. No, I won't." Tears briefly glinted in her eyes before she blinked them away.

Sam sighed. "You can't avenge your uncle if you're dead."

Amber scowled but retreated to the cab of the truck. Sam turned to James. "All right." The old soldier's voice was low now, as though he was afraid he'd be overheard. "I'm going to plant the Claymore. You'd better watch me. You might need to do it your own self."

James' hands trembled around the shotgun. He swallowed. Sam went and unhooked the back gate. He lowered it slowly rather than letting it fall. A brief relief welled up inside James. The less noise, the better. He watched as Sam retrieved the lethal trio of mines, the AR-15, and a megaphone, of all things. He hadn't noticed *that* in the truck bed. His gaze drifted back toward Amber. Of course, he'd been a bit preoccupied...

Then Sam turned to James and Amber. "Quiet now. This is life or death."

The lump in James' throat was so huge it must look like a tumor. James slowly nodded. Sam set off toward the two totem poles. His legs made of lead, James followed.

As they drew near the towering icons, James' hands trembled. They were going into the lair of something terrible and unholy. Could those mines kill it? Were they walking to their deaths?

He looked up at the totem poles. The azure eyes watched him like a hawk regarding a mouse. He suddenly wanted to run. Run back to the truck, toss Amber in with him, and get the hell out. He didn't want to follow Sam into hell.

He swallowed. *No way.* The bastards kidnapped Dad. They intended to kill him in one of the most hideous ways imaginable. His grip tightened on his shotgun. He would save him or die trying.

Sam passed beneath the totem poles. James quickened his step ever so slightly. Every scrape of his foot against the gravel roared in his ears. The cultists *had* to hear them coming.

James kept his eyes locked on Sam and the trail ahead. The path bent ahead, twisting around a large bush whose leaves were fringed with brown rot. In the distance, voices murmured. The cult was here, all gathered to watch Dad offered to a monstrosity.

James grit his teeth. Over their dead bodies. Over his dead body if necessary, but over their dead bodies first.

The murmuring grew louder as they approached the bush and the scattering of stunted plants surrounding it. Beyond it dozens of people, mostly men but a few women, gathered in ranks almost like a military parade. Several wore the brown of the Sheriff's Office. Those men had to be armed. Even if they weren't, there were too many for him and Sam to handle even with their guns. James' gaze drifted over to the bush and its companions. The vegetation might hide them from the cultists. Emphasis on *might*.

Sam brought a finger to his thin lips. He walked up to the bush and set one of the Claymores on the ground, embedding its spiky legs into the wet earth.

James' eyes bulged. "Wait," he whispered. "You set that thing off, and Dad's out there, you might kill him!"

Sam shook his head. "If they've got him on the table, he's too far away." He paused. "If we're late, he's almost certainly there. Phil will want to make a big entrance."

James swallowed. The man had fought in an actual war. Surely he knew what he was talking about. But if he was wrong, Dad might die.

Sam knelt by the curving mine and adjusted it slightly.

Aiming it. James filed that bit away for later. He didn't know how well these things could be aimed. He did his best to divide his attention between the cultists and Sam. He'd need to know how these things worked, just in case, but he also wanted to be the first to know if the cultists spotted them.

Sam plugged the long nose of one end of the cord into the mine and crept backward across the muddy, leafy ground. James moved with him, looking back and forth between Sam and the horde of cultists gathering nearby. The lump in his throat returned. If someone heard them rustling around and the mine wasn't ready, they were dog meat.

Sam backed up about sixty feet. He plugged the tail end of the cable into a small box-like device. James narrowed his eyes. That must be the detonator.

"Hold this," Sam ordered. "Don't you *dare* squeeze it until I tell you." He paused. "But when the time comes, you might need to squeeze it up to three times. Build up a charge to blow it." He slung the AR-15 strap over his shoulder and picked the bullhorn off the ground.

James' jaw dropped. Was he planning on warning them? Best set off the mine and be done with it!

Before he could stop him, Sam brought the megaphone to his lips.

———

Phillip stood in the shadows beneath the trees, the assembled congregants barely visible through the tangled underbrush. The earth was wet beneath his booted feet, wet and warm. It crawled with the creatures He permitted in His holy dwelling, *alive*.

As was the man spread-eagled and buck naked on the picnic table in the shadow of the bell that would call Him to feed. Phillip's lip curled in contempt. From the report of those who'd taken him, he hadn't put up much of a fight at all. And his son, the real target, had been found cowering in a closet. Found by Sam no less.

A smile kinked his lips. He'd need to call off Reed. The Army puke had done good after all. There'd been some long-haired motorcycle fiend he'd had in his company he'd have sworn would have buggered off to some boom-boom house in Saigon at first chance, but the man had earned a Bronze Star at Con Thien in '68. Sam had well and truly exceeded his expectations, just like that hippie had.

He was glad hadn't condemned Sam to the same traitor's death he'd helped carry out decades before. The younger man had shown his worth.

Phillip looked at his watch. Where *was* Sam? He'd have liked to sacrifice them together, the father and the son. It'd be fitting. Two carpetbaggers, one sacrifice. He would be pleased and sated for a time. And the stranger in black wouldn't be able to learn anything he shouldn't from the boy.

He shook his head. The lord of the wet wood would linger after eating the father. The boy would feed Him soon enough. Phillip chuckled at the thought. The boy had thought he'd escaped that afternoon. He hadn't reckoned that He had men and women serving as His hands and feet outside the woods.

Phillip stepped to the edge of the pond and drew his knife. A quick slice and the red blood dripped bright from his hand into the dark waters. He would smell the blood. He would come. The high priest smiled.

A voice sounded in the distance, interrupting his joy. An amplified, electronic voice. He couldn't make out the words, but it sounded familiar even though it was coming from a megaphone. He stepped forward, boots popping free from the dark mud. They'd never used instruments to praise Him, let alone electronic ones.

————

"ALL RIGHT, EVERYBODY." James' head snapped in the direction of the cultists. The evil throng turned their way, surprise written on their many faces. "You all are fixing to commit another murder, and I'm not going to have it."

"Brother Sam, what the hell are you doing?" someone called out. "And who's that with you?"

"The Edington cops are on their way," Sam continued. "But y'all have enough time to get the hell out of here if you stop what you're doing right now!"

James nearly snapped his fingers. Sam had been a cult member for years. Many of these people were his friends. Of course he wasn't going to blow them all to hell and gone!

He looked down to the detonator in his hands. Of course, he could set it off himself. Kill them before they drew guns of their own or straight-up charged. Sam's kindness might get them both killed. His hand tightened on the detonator. Best not take any chances.

He shook his head. Dad was probably out there somewhere. He didn't want to destroy the cult if he killed Dad too. He loosened his grip on the detonator. He wouldn't set the mine off without Sam's permission.

But he *would* keep an eye on the cultists. Sam might be so busy talking he might not notice if they tried something.

"The man on the table belongs to Him now!" someone shouted back. "The time for mercy has passed!" The voice softened. "Brother Sam, you know that."

So Dad *was* on the table. Thank God. If the table was far

enough away, that shouldn't be a problem. His hand tightened on the detonator once again.

"I have a bomb on the edge of the clearing," Sam continued. Muttering erupted amidst the crowd. "My friend here has the trigger. Y'all have to the count of ten to clear out. Go out through the woods, come around to your cars, and y'all get gone!"

That got James' attention. Sam didn't seem to have thought that one through. Unless Amber jumped back in the car immediately, they'd see her. If they had any brains, they'd try to take her hostage to force him and Sam to stand down. Or maybe they'd just kill her out of spite. That seemed like the kind of thing they'd do.

James watched the crowd. Sweat beaded on his forehead. He looked down at the detonator in his hand. If they decided to jump ship, he was going to make sure they didn't pull anything once they got to their cars. Sam could take care of Dad. A couple looked to be edging toward the trees lining the far side of the clearing. Good. Maybe more would follow. Hope rose in his chest, pushing away his fear for Amber. Maybe they wouldn't need to use the mines. Maybe this could all be ended peacefully.

Then James spotted a big man edging through the crowd. The man's hand was inside his jacket. His heart sank. That had to be a gun under there.

Looks like the whole "my friend will set the bomb off" thing isn't going to protect Sam.

James' hand started to shake around the detonator. Sam had risked everything to save his life and do the same for Dad. James had thought he'd do the same for him. But as the cultist crept nearer, it became more and more obvious he might actually have to do it. Failing would be too horrific to contemplate.

"Sam," James hissed. "On your right. There's a man with a gun."

Sam nodded to James slightly. "One," he began. "Two. Three."

James kept his eyes locked on the armed cultist. The big man was close to the front now. People were pulling away to let him pass. They knew what the bastard was going to do. That'd make it all right for him to blow them all to hell.

"Don't listen to him!" someone called out from amidst the cultists. "How do we know he's even got a bomb?"

"Four. Five."

The man was at the front of the crowd now. He was taller than Sam. Wider too. His eyes were cold, cold as ice. Was that Phil, the one Sam and Amber were talking about? He looked ruthless enough.

His hand emerged from the jacket. He definitely had a gun, a shiny black pistol. The weapon rose in his hand, a trajectory that'd bring it to bear on Sam's head.

"Six."

"Sam!" James hissed. "Gun!"

"Even if there is a bomb," someone else shouted. "He will protect us! He always has!"

The gun was almost there. Nobody had left the clearing. More people were edging forward. Fear twisted like a coiling snake in James' gut. They were pretty obviously going to charge once the armed man pulled the trigger. They'd swarm him and pull him down. Then he'd be lucky if they just beat him to death. More than likely he'd be offered up to that *thing* right beside Dad.

Sam ducked. The man pulled the trigger. The gunshot barked loud in the gloom. Wood splintered from a tree near where Sam's head had been.

"James, now!"

James obeyed.

———

THUNDER CRACKED. It didn't just crack. It roared like a tornado, consuming every other sound in the sanctuary. Smoke rolled forward to engulf the congregation, but not before Phillip could see bloody flowers bloom on the faces and bodies of the congregants. The harsh stink of explosives rolled over him along with the screams.

He knew the sound. He'd used that weapon before.

"Claymore," he snarled aloud. "Claymore directional mine!"

Who would dare attack His lair with Claymores? If this was the EPD—he had full faith in the loyalty of the Sheriff's Office—leaving their jurisdiction to arrogantly challenge Him on His own ground, they'd start out with flash-bangs and gas. They wouldn't kill immediately. Not even if they had the man in black to spur them on.

Edington. His heart sank. The EPD and the civilians they protected would find out soon that their handguns, their rifles, and even that armored personnel carrier with the .50 cal they bought with that damned federal anti-drug money were *nothing* compared to Him. He was older than the white men, older than the red men, perhaps even older than men, period. He would laugh at their attempts to destroy Him, laugh as He killed them all and made Edington like Sodom and Gomorrah. Even if the stranger promised them federal assistance, his promises were a broken staff that would wound any foolish enough to lean on them.

Phillip's eyes swept the sanctuary now profaned with the blood and steaming guts of his followers. An all-too-familiar smell of shit from bellies blown open mingled with the sulfurous stink of spent explosives. Even now, decades after he'd first gone to war, the smell could still turn his stomach. Occasional moans touched his ears. No one rose from the red massacre.

"No," he whispered. The congregation was gone. All dead, or soon to be. All dead except for him.

His gaze turned to the man on the table. His chest still rose and fell. His head turned away, his eyes no doubt drinking the scene of slaughter. The carpetbagger had seen the elephant. A pity he'd die soon anyway.

Phillip would speak to the police when they came. He'd warn them of their sin and then summon Him. The carpetbagger's death—and the death of the stranger if he was with them—would seal the EPD to Him, as the deaths of slaves had sealed the first white congregants to Him hundreds of years ago.

The congregation would go on. Edington would go on.

———

A WAVE of gray smoke consumed the sanctuary, reaching back toward Sam and James like a giant clutching hand. James looked away, but he couldn't ignore the sounds of agony from the clearing. He trembled, stomach boiling. If he'd eaten anything heavier than that ice cream he'd had with Amber, he'd have puked by now. He prayed the bodies of the cultists had shielded Dad from the waves of ball bearings blasting out of the Claymore like an enormous shotgun.

James looked down at the detonator in his hands. He'd done it. He'd just killed God knows how many people. This wasn't *Call of Duty*. This wasn't *HALO*. This wasn't even paintball with its bruises. This was *real*. His face grew hot with shame. Tears began building in his eyes.

He blinked back the tears. His trembling hand clenched

into a fist around the detonator. This was *war*. The monster they worshiped had attacked him and murdered Bill. The cultists had attacked his family. The abomination they worshiped had no doubt been killing people for centuries. And now, finally, somebody was striking back. A grin split his face.

He set the detonator on the ground and picked up the shotgun. The smoke was starting to clear, rising up into the choking canopy and revealing the carnage the Claymore had left behind.

Where there'd once been living men and women now were only heaps of mangled bodies. The closer to the mine, the more the bodies looked like ground beef at the grocery store. Blood pooled on the dark earth amidst the mounds of mutilated flesh. The air was thick with the smell of massacre, of coppery blood and strangely enough, shit. His stomach surged into his mouth. He swallowed vomit tasting of mingled chocolate and peanut butter before he could make a spectacle of himself.

James looked beyond the field of slaughter to where the picnic table had been. Where was it? Where was Dad?

He soon had his answer. The picnic table was still there. A naked white body was splayed across it. Although James couldn't be sure, the hair color and height looked a lot like Dad. Though bloodied bodies lay on the ground within feet of the picnic table, the sacrificial victim was unmarred.

Oh thank you God.

James leaped up. "Wait!" Sam shouted. But James was already running through the vegetation that had sheltered them from the backblast, heedless of the danger of any armed survivor, heedless of the squishing of his shoes in the bloodied earth or the opened guts of the cultists.

———

Rage boiled deep inside Phillip as the tall youth with dark hair and freckles rushed across the clearing. He had bandages over his left cheek. It was the boy! Phillip looked for the stranger in the dark suit, but he was nowhere to be seen. This wasn't possible. How had the boy who'd fled Him managed to do this?

Phillip's hand fell to his service pistol. He would punish the brat for this insolence, punish him like his foolish parents who no doubt wanted to be his "friend" never had. His hand trembled with anger around the weapon's pebbled grip.

He didn't draw, even though he could probably hit the boy from where he was. The little carpetbagger shit had to have help, even if it wasn't the EPD. Perhaps the stranger in black had put him up to this. Phillip kept his eye on the boy and waited for whoever helped the little bastard to reveal themselves.

———

Warm wetness swallowed James' foot. He looked down. He'd stepped into the open guts of Deputy Bowie, the one who'd tried to convince him Bill had taken a knife to his face. The stink of shit rose around him. The huge man moaned.

"Holy fuck!" James screamed. He jumped nearly a foot. Something warm against his ankle came with him. The man screamed this time. It was only when he'd gotten both feet back on the wet ground that he saw he'd brought a loop of the man's intestine with him. James screamed again and again, uncaring of how he looked, yanking the intestine still further. The deputy's screams echoed his own. James finally kicked his foot free.

Then he stumbled and spewed his partially-digested choco-late-peanut butter ice cream over the wet ground. He imagined

Sam looking on with disapproval. He was glad Amber wasn't there to see him look like a wimp.

He dragged himself to his feet. Time to be strong. For Dad. "Dad!" James shouted. "DAD!"

His father's head snapped in his direction. "James?" he asked. "James, what are you doing here? Did they take you too? Did they bring you here?"

"No! I've come to save you." He ran, ignoring the wet warmth clinging to his ankle and the last bodies squishing beneath his feet.

He stopped short. Dad was tied down to the picnic table, and James didn't have anything to cut with. And he was suddenly much more aware of his father's nudity.

I really, really don't want to see Dad's junk.

Studiously avoiding his father's groin as much as he could, James looked Dad over. A few small wounds marred him, but it looked like the cultists had taken the brunt of the Claymore.

Good. Bastards deserved it.

James stepped forward. Even without his pocketknife, how hard could it be to untie the leather straps? Once he got one arm free, Dad could help him. They'd be done pretty darn quick, and then they could get the hell out of there.

"Halt!" a hard voice snarled. "Stop right there!" James' head snapped in the direction of the sound.

A robed man ran out of the woods, out from under trees that had crept up to an ancient, heavy bell. Iron-gray hair cut close to his skull peeked out from under his hood. Gray eyes alight with rage focused on James. And so was the shiny black pistol in his hands.

"You," he spat. "You thought you'd pulled a fast one, didn't you?"

James still had the shotgun, but there was no way he could

raise it before the man fired. His only hope was to keep the man talking so Sam could blow the bastard's head off.

"Yeah," James declared, hoping the man couldn't detect the trembling in his voice. "Yeah, I did. I'm the one who just wiped your little cult off the map." James swallowed. "That was me. I was the one who pressed the big red button. I killed all of you... you inbred cocksuckers. Probably improved the gene pool around here."

The cult leader's lips peeled back from his white teeth. "James," Dad warned.

"Mind your manners, *boy*," the cult leader snarled. He glared at James. "How the hell did you manage this?" He gestured at the carnage all around. "You city kids don't know how to do jack shit. You stay inside all day because you've got no yards and playing in the street's too dangerous—"

"He wasn't alone, Phil," Sam interrupted. Both James' and Phil's heads snapped toward the far edge of the clearing. Sam came walking toward them, red blood soaking his jeans up to his knees. The AR-15 was in his hands. He had a pair of camouflage pants balled up under his arm.

Shock, anger, and more than a little fear flooded Phil's face. "Sam Dixon, you goddamn *traitor*! It had to be you! How else could this brat get hold of a fucking Claymore?"

James nearly jumped. How did the cult leader know they'd used Claymores? If he could figure that out, anybody coming on the scene later would. He and Sam had planned to rescue Dad but hadn't really thought about what would come next. Especially with how tight the cult was with the Sheriff's Office. They'd go right to the Guard armory, and that'd lead them straight to Sam.

"Yeah," Sam said. "Yeah, it was me. You said all this was for the protection of Edington, but all you've been doing is trying to feed innocent folk to a monster!"

"Don't call Him that!" Phil snarled back. "Don't you *dare*!"

"That's what He is, ain't He?" Sam challenged. "God doesn't need human meat to live." He drew a breath. "That thing's no god. Don't know what the hell it is, but it's not Him. Not at all."

Phil's gun hand whipped away from James. Sam snapped up the AR-15.

———

AMBER LOOKED over her shoulder toward the road that brought them to the cult's inner sanctum for the third or fourth time since the Claymore's roar and the butchered cultists' screams savaged her eardrums. Still, nobody came from the entrance to the tree farm. Her head snapped back toward the path leading into the trees. James and Sam were off confronting only God knew what to save James' dad from the gang of murderers who'd gone unpunished for far too long and she was out here gathering moss.

Somebody's got to watch the car, she told herself. *They might need to get away in a hurry.* If they rescued James' father but couldn't escape the cult's "sanctuary," whatever cultists remained might overwhelm them. And then there was the monstrosity they worshiped. A lump gathered in her throat. The uncle she'd never met had died by inches, slowly devoured by something terrible. Her father had never told her much, but her imagination could fill in the details. Something huge and black and brimming with eyes and arms and teeth. The bastards no doubt made a production of it, with torches and drums like the heathen savages they were underneath their polite exteriors.

She shook her head. James and Sam needed her to keep a clear head. The bastards by the front gate couldn't be allowed anywhere near the car. And she had a damn good idea of what they'd do to her for daring to challenge them—before they fed her to the monster like they did her uncle.

She looked back at the road leading out of the tree farm. Nothing moved. There wasn't even the bouncing, crumpling sound of wheels on gravel. Nobody was coming. She returned her attention to the path leading between the two towering evil statues. Their multitude of azure eyes regarded her like a big fish might regard a little one.

She shook her head again. She wasn't some foolish woman who'd lose her head when left alone. She had a job, and she was going to do it, fears be damned. James and Sam were fine. There hadn't been any noise since the single gunshot and the Claymore's explosion. Perhaps they'd killed all of the cultists at once. The thought brought a most unladylike grin to her face. The only ones left to fear were those yahoos by the gate.

Gunshots cracked through the trees. Amber snapped her shotgun to her shoulder, looking down the length of the barrel like she was tracking a turkey by the reservoir. She stepped toward the path leading into the cult's inner sanctum but quickly stopped herself.

If James and Sam still lived, they'd need her to make sure they could get the hell out of there.

———

THE GUNSHOTS OVERLAPPED, cracking like whips in James' ears. Sam toppled backward. Phil staggered like he'd been hit with a sledgehammer. A flower of red blood bloomed on his right shoulder, turning his gray robes black as it spread. But he was still up and still in control of his weapon

Oh shit!

James had only one chance. He raised the shotgun as fast as

he could. "Lights out," he snarled, hoping he sounded scary and not about to shit himself.

Phil's gun swung toward James. James squeezed his eyes shut and pulled the trigger. The shotgun kicked against his shoulder like one of the tougher kids he'd sparred with at Choi Kwong Do. The blast bit painfully loud in his ears. The recoil sent him staggering, but it'd done worse to the cult leader.

Phil's face above the nose was gone. Gray brain matter decorated the carved black wood holding up the iron bell. Chunks of white skull slid down the post made slick with blood and brain, the ones the shot hadn't sunk into the wooden flesh like daggers. He could see the shiny inner surface of what was left of the man's skull. The shot had quite literally blown the cult leader's brains out.

The more he stared at his ghoulish handiwork, the more his hands shook. The weight of what he'd done pressed down on him. He'd just killed God knew how many people with a land mine and then went and shot a man. James looked behind him at the mangled corpses littering the clearing and quickly looked away, only for his eyes to fall back on the corpse of the cult leader.

"James," a pain-ridden voice said. "James, listen to me." James' head snapped up, eyes bulging. Sam had managed to pull himself onto his knees. "We've got to get your pa out of here."

How was he up and moving? The way he fell, he must've been shot square in the chest. Was he wearing body armor? If he was, did he have another set he could have shared? James shook his head. No time to wonder about that. They had to get Dad out of there before the Edington cops showed up. If they were gone and the cops found the field of slaughter, they'd have a chance. It didn't look like there were any living witnesses.

Sam pulled himself up, grimacing all the while. He stumbled forward, catching himself on the table. "You get his hands. I'll get his feet."

James stepped around Sam. His fingers leaped to the leather ropes crucifying Dad against the wood. He tugged at the bonds. The leather was wet. Untying him would be a pain in the ass.

After what felt like an eternity of tugging and scrabbling, he managed to pull one strand out of the knot. Slowly, too slowly, he drew the strand free. After that, it was easy to untie the rest. Dad's hand flew to the other rope binding his wrist. A moment later Sam got one foot free.

"Did they ring the bell?" Sam demanded as Dad rose to his feet. "Did they ring the bell?"

"No," Dad said. "Not that I can remember."

"Good. If they didn't, we might still have some time. We've got to get the hell out of here. The congregants at the front of the farm might've heard the Claymore go off. They're probably on their way in now. We'd best not be here when they get there."

James heard everything Sam said, but his attention was on the pond. The water was moving. He could see the faintest glow of azure light. It was getting brighter.

James' grip tightened on the shotgun, but that didn't stop his hands from trembling. Bile started rising into his throat, even though there couldn't possibly anything left in it.

"Sam. Sam. We've got a bigger problem."

CHAPTER FIFTEEN

JAMES POINTED TO THE POND. THE LIGHTS GREW brighter. The surface bulged. Water lapped at the edges. Something big was coming up. And James knew just what it was.

Sam's eyes widened in his narrow face. "Oh *shit.*" He looked straight at James. "Run. Run right fucking *now!*"

James didn't need any more encouragement. The three ran, Dad halfway into the pants Sam had brought him. It wasn't far to where they'd parked. Get in the truck and get the hell out of there. He'd outrun the monster on an ATV. They could definitely get out of there in a pickup. Wet flesh and warm bloody earth squished beneath James' feet. He nearly tripped over a tall skinny man in a coat and tie whose left half was shredded. He didn't care. All that mattered was *running.*

Wood splintered behind them. James knew he shouldn't look back. Just keep running, run, run, run...

But he looked back. And he wished he hadn't.

The thing in the woods rose out of its watery lair, its tentacles looping around tree limbs.

172 MATTHEW W. QUINN

Oh, my sweet God. It's even bigger than I thought.

He'd seen the head and the first set of arms during the ATV race, but that wasn't half of it. No, more like a third of it. The sinuous vastness kept pushing out of the pond, more tentacles lashing out to seize tree limbs and pull its bulk upward. Its enormous weight settled on the edge of the water, pushing up ridges of mud. Water cascaded down its sides like waterfalls and spilled across the clearing, thinning the pools of red blood.

The huge azure eyes swept the sanctuary, growing slightly larger as they took in the scene of slaughter. It crawled into the clearing like a huge snake from its hole, its bulk casting a shadow over the place of sacrifice now sodden with the blood of its worshippers. Its long tentacles reached out, first poking at Phil's near-headless corpse. The first thought that rose to James' mind was a dog discovering its master was dead.

The creature looked up, its gaze following the bodies as they radiated away from where it had been offered human sacrifices for God knows how long. Any moment now, it'd catch sight of them.

"Move!" James snarled. "Now! Before it sees us!"

That got the trio moving, but it was too late. The monstrosity opened its enormous mouth and roared.

———

It had been a long time since the gunshots. Amber couldn't hear anything from the sanctuary.

Her grip tightened on her shotgun. She threw a glance over her shoulder. The road leading back to the tree farm entrance was where the danger would come from. There were congregants—probably armed congregants—at the entrance. Her job was to guard the truck. The cultist guards were the immediate danger.

But what if James and Sam didn't come back with James' dad? Sam had told her to run, but didn't give her any more instructions. Her jaw tightened. He was the trained soldier, not her. He would know when to stand one's ground and when to cut and run. The mine had gone off—half the county could've probably heard *that*—and then the gunshots. And then nothing. Her mind whirled. If there were gunshots after the mine went off, that meant James and Sam weren't killed by their own weapon. Did they kill surviving cultists? Or were they wounded and did surviving cultists kill them?

She brought her shotgun to her shoulder and pointed it down the trail into hell. If any cultists came from that direction, she wanted to be able to hit them right away. The turkeys she'd hunted at the reservoir were innocent. Anybody worshiping the thing in the woods was most assuredly *not*.

As she stood with her gun pointing between the two statues, her gaze wandered over to them. Her stomach twisted inside her as she looked at the two mock-ups of the horror worshiped in the sanctuary beyond. The horror that ate her uncle from his feet up.

A shiver ran through her. If the abomination was anything like those totem poles, she didn't want to see it. Ever.

The silence oppressed her. She swallowed. Where were James and Sam? If the cultists killed them, they'd be coming after her next. But nobody, friend or foe, came through the gap between the totem poles. Was everybody dead, like the end of that awful movie she'd heard about where three tourists were made into a centipede?

Then an ear-shattering roar like a dinosaur from a movie cracked the gloom. Amber jumped, nearly dropping the gun. There were black bears in the rural parts of the county, but she'd never heard one roar like that. There was only one thing around here that could possibly make a noise like that. Only one.

Fear rolled throughout her body, setting sweat beading on her brow. She could get in the truck and drive away. Even if it came hunting for her, she could outrun it. James had on the ATV, after all.

She breathed in and out. To hell with running away. Her kin didn't leave Edington even though the cult murdered her uncle. She wasn't going to leave James and Sam to die like her uncle had at the hands—tentacles—of some monster.

Gripping her weapon tightly, she set off toward the sanctuary.

———

The monster roared. James grit his teeth at the pain in his ears. His legs suddenly turned to jelly. He stumbled. He remembered Bill dying on the abomination's claws, his pushing the ATV accelerator the way down to get away. And pissing himself.

Luckily he didn't feel the need to do that just now.

Suddenly Amber came around the bend, a shotgun in her hands. James tried to stop himself. Gravel flew, but he still slammed into her anyway. They both tumbled into the mud. The shotgun flew from James' hands.

Sam was almost on top of them when James pulled himself to his feet. Amber wasn't far behind him.

"Amber!" Sam demanded. "What the hell?"

"I heard gunshots!" she said. "Then nothing. Then the roar. I..." Her voice trailed away. Her eyes bulged. Her jaw worked silently. James knew at long last she'd set her eyes upon the thing that killed her uncle, the thing the cult she feared worshiped.

"Sam!" James interrupted. "Claymore!" He didn't know whether or not the mine could actually hurt something that damn big, but it was worth a shot. Sam had left the mines by the bush when he'd confronted Phil. They were right there, ready to be planted.

Sam had his AR-15 shouldered. "You plant it! You saw what I did!"

"Got it!" The words were out of James' mouth before he really had time to think. He *had* seen how Sam had set the mine, but the memory ran away, driven by mind-shaking fear. The rifle popped, but the monster didn't even flinch.

Hands trembling, James took up the mine. He looked up. The monster was advancing now, its bulk pushing aside the mangled cultists. One man moaned before the train of black flesh rolled over him. Sam kept firing. Turquoise rivulets ran from the holes he'd punched in the monster's skin, but the abomination wasn't even slowing down.

"James! Now!" Sam demanded. He pointed at Dad. "Amber, you get him out of here!"

While Amber and Dad ran one way, James ran the opposite. He jammed the mine into the wet ground between the bush and a mangled cultist. That one looked almost like his grandmother. He looked away and busied himself plugging the detonator cable into the mine.

Something deeper than the AR-15 shouted behind him. He glanced back. Amber and her shotgun had joined the party. She must've sent Dad on toward the car. Without a gun of his own, there wasn't much he could do anyway.

He looked forward. The monster was coming straight at him, rolling like a wave of lava. A multitude of eyes locked on him.

"Yeah, you bastard!" James shouted at it. "I'm the one that got away! You miss me?"

The eyes narrowed. James suddenly needed to piss. The thing understood him. It was intelligent.

As if things couldn't get any worse.

James jammed the other end of the cord into the detonator. He didn't have time to aim. The thing was so damn big it wasn't like he really needed to.

The cable spilled away as James scampered back, bending it around the bush. Amber quickly joined him. Only Sam stayed where he was. James didn't know how far back the explosion would reach, but he was pretty sure it'd hit Sam.

"Come on!" James shouted.

Sam picked up the last Claymore and ran. He didn't get far when a huge black tentacle struck like a scorpion tail, burying a hooked claw into his shoulder. The blow slammed him into the mud just beyond the dying bush. The Claymore flew out of his hands, landing a few feet away from James.

Amber shouldered the shotgun again. The weapon boomed in James' right ear. The tentacle flinched. Turquoise blood burst from many small wounds. James got the idea immediately. He pumped the forearm handle to spit out the casing from the shell that killed Phil and brought the weapon to his shoulder. No hesitation this time, not with the monster. Thunder cracked. The shotgun slammed into his shoulder, knocking him back a step. But the trickle of blood was now a pour. He and Amber must've hit something important.

Amber fired again as the tentacle started pulling Sam back. Then she threw the shotgun aside and ran toward Sam.

"Stay back!" Sam shouted. He buried his hands in the wet ground. The tentacle pulled taut. Sam screamed. James aimed again, trying to line up the shotgun with where the unholy limb was bloodiest while not hitting Amber. He'd blow the bastard's arm clean off.

With a wet tearing sound that made James sick to his stomach, the tentacle came apart where they'd hit it. Sam dragged himself forward, shirt soaked with mingled red and turquoise blood and what was left of the tentacle hanging off his back.

Then Dad appeared from behind them. He ran up and grabbed Sam's hands, pulling him away from the monster. They'd barely gotten a few feet when even more tentacles lashed out. Another hooked claw buried itself in Sam's back. Dad threw himself out of the way. The tentacle that would have speared him instead slammed into his side, sending him sprawling. He crawled toward James and Amber as the tentacle hoisted Sam in the air.

Just like Bill.

No, it wasn't just like Bill. James had no weapon then. Now he had the Claymore detonator in his hands, and Sam floated out of the line of fire. James had just a moment before the tentacle would drag Sam into its huge mouth.

"James!" Sam shouted. "Blow the Claymore! Kill it now!"

He snatched up the detonator and squeezed the trigger.

Nothing happened. His heart leaped into his throat. Did something come loose when he was unspooling the cable? If the problem was the end plugged into the mine, they were screwed, but if it was the end plugged into the trigger?

He jammed the cord and trigger together. The tentacle holding Sam pulled him toward the slavering mouth with far too many sharp teeth. James pumped the trigger once, twice, three times.

Light flashed. James looked away. The terrible roar drove blades of pain into his ears. Despite the distance and the bush, the claymore's backblast rolled over him, nearly knocking him onto his ass in the mud. Something wet and hot slammed into his face, soaking through the bandage to burn in the wound the creature had left on his cheek. Amber and Dad cried out in pain beside him. A quick glance saw blood on their faces and clothes, but not much.

"It's hurt!" Amber shouted. James finally dared to look. He gasped.

The thing wallowed amid the broken and shattered bodies of its worshipers. Glowing blue-green blood, so much like its terrible eyes, covered its black skin. The blood pumped from hundreds of wounds the Claymore had torn into its shiny black flesh. Steaming fluids cascaded from pulped eyes. Still-living tentacles writhed on the muddy ground, dragging themselves away from the monster they'd been torn from as they grasped reflexively.

Movement in front of the monster seized James' attention. Someone tried to push themselves up amid the welter of human and monstrous gore. Blood matted the man's red hair and the camouflage he wore. It was Sam! James had been too slow. He'd been caught in the blast.

———

SAM'S CHEST still ached from Phil's gunshot. Now his legs and behind burned with pain. He pulled himself up on both arms, ignoring the burning any movement brought. One of his black boots lay ahead. The boot was full of meat. Sam tried to wriggle his toes. It worked for his left foot, however much the pain nearly blinded him. But nothing at all on his right.

He looked behind him. His right leg was gone below mid-shin. The damn blue-on-blue he'd thought he'd left behind in the Gulf had taken his damn foot. Anger rose in him. He shook his head.

Serves me right for worshipping the damn monster all these

*years, helping offer folk to it. Standing by when Leroy Tolliver
was offered up to it...*

Sam shook his head. He had more immediate problems. He
looked up. The movement jolted the two claws buried in his
back, sending waves of pain throughout his torso. One arm gave
out. He fell down into the mud. His chin slammed into the
ground. He momentarily saw black. Ignoring the pain as best
he could, he kept his attention locked on the monstrosity in
front of him.

The thing lay there amid the bloody clearing. The only
movement was from some tentacles ripped away by the explosion, still clutching dead men or each other. The movement
slowed as the last life left them.

Had James killed it? That'd serve Phil right. The thing he'd
thought was a god, killing by good old-fashioned American
know-how and one of the city kids he hated so much. He
pushed himself back up on his elbows, despite the pain and the
weight of the severed tentacles. The creature lay unmoving in
front of him, blood trickling from its many wounds.

Sam laughed. Maybe they were getting out of this alive
after all. He'd need to be fitted with a fake lower leg, but a lot of
the boys coming back from Iraq and Afghanistan had those.
They didn't seem *too* bad off.

Then the monster twitched. Sam's heart sank. It wasn't
over yet.

Several eyes in the midst of its bulk rolled open wide and
staring. Its vast jaws parted. Many teeth hung from tendrils of
black flesh, but still more were firmly embedded in its maw.
Several tentacles, claws gone but still attached to its body,
worked their way across the wet ground.

Where was his rifle? He tore his attention away from the
mouth big enough to swallow a car. If he could get some shots
into its open mouth, maybe it'd damage something vital. Back

in the Gulf, there'd been a showoff sniper who'd shot an Iraqi through his open mouth. The bullet had punched through the poor conscript's brain stem. Maybe there was something similar in the monstrosity.

There! His rifle lay in the mud to his right. He reached for it, wincing at every movement. His hand closed around the cold metal stock. When he pulled, the barrel and magazine came away. The blast had shattered his weapon more thoroughly than it had his body.

Well son of a bitch. Sam wasn't going to be able to do anything anytime soon, and the monster was recovering.

Its remaining eyes locked on him, glaring like someone bigger he'd gotten a lucky hit on and pissed off. Fear sent waves of trembling through his body, the pain making him see red.

"The Lord is my shepherd," he whispered. Hot blood dripped from his mouth to spatter on his hands. "I shall not want..."

The abomination he'd once worshiped charged.

———

James screamed wordlessly. The monster surged toward Sam, its glowing blood soaking the ground around it. Sam didn't have time to scream before the enormous mouth engulfed him. The thing threw its head back like an alligator on Animal Planet. When it opened its mouth to spew mud and grass, the detritus was soaked with mingled blood, both human and monstrous.

He snatched up the shotgun and pulled the trigger. This time he held it properly, and the recoil wasn't too bad. With a scream of rage, Amber fired too.

The creature reared like a cobra and swung its huge head to

face them. Most of its eyes were gone, but the remaining ones burned with rage.

James looked to the last Claymore near his feet. He hoped nothing important was damaged. Gripping the shotgun with one hand, he ran forward and snatched it up.

"Get to the cars!" Dad interrupted. "It's hurt! That'll slow it down!"

James didn't need any encouragement. The three ran just as the monster surged their way. The sound of its bulk sliding along the ground thundered in his ears. He threw a glance behind him. Wounded as it was, it was still pretty damn fast.

The path curved ahead. It wasn't far to the cars.

"Through the trees!" James shouted. They could move between the trees. It—probably—couldn't.

Dad and Amber turned left, abandoning the path to pass under the pines. James followed. The thing roared behind them. Wood cracked. A quick glance showed clawed tentacles sinking into the pine trees' flesh. James swallowed. The thing wasn't going to let the woods slow it down, not for long.

They quickly passed through the woods into the parking lot. There they ran into more trouble. Two more cultists were getting out of an old blue sedan. Both were armed. One pointed a long finger at James.

"It's that kid!"

The other, shorter and uglier, raised some kind of rifle. James didn't have time to aim his shotgun. He wasn't even sure if he had any shells left in the gun and he didn't have time to get any of the shells from his pocket.

Amber's shotgun roared beside him. The glass in the open car door exploded almost musically. The armed cultist flew backward onto the gravel. The other ducked behind the open car door.

James looked behind him. The creature's huge blackness

pushed through the trees. Glowing turquoise blood trickled between the pine trees' scales. Its remaining eyes locked on them like those of an obsessed madman.

"Get down!" Dad threw himself atop James. The two tumbled, the rough gravel stabbing at James' bare arms. A gunshot cracked a moment later.

"Amber!" James shouted.

"I'm fine!" she shouted back. A shotgun blast emphasized her point.

James lay on his side facing the cultists' car. He had the perfect shot at the survivor's legs. He pulled the trigger and hoped he wasn't empty.

The shotgun boomed. The blast blew the man's legs out from under him. There was a scream and a thud as the man toppled headfirst into the other side of the door.

Before James could laugh at the absurdity of the situation, the thing roared. His head snapped toward the sound. The monstrosity was almost to the parking lot, murder in its remaining eyes. James looked from it to the cultists' car. The bastards should have their keys. They could get in and drive away.

"Dad, Amber!" He pointed to the car.

Dad had barely gotten off him when police sirens filled the air. What were the cops doing here? Did the cultists call before they came to investigate? Were the police coming to take revenge on those who dared defy their god and kill their kin?

Well, to hell with that. If James, Dad, and Amber were going to die like the Union cavalry and God knew how many others, he'd damn sure drag the thing in the woods into hell with him. He threw the near-useless shotgun aside, picked up the Claymore, and headed for the trees. Every instinct told him to run. He shook his head. He showed that thing his back, he'd get a claw through it just like Bill, and now Sam, had. And if

Dad and Amber hadn't gotten the car started, they were dead too.

The thing drew closer, its remaining eyes bright in the shadow of the trees. It'd soon have a clear shot, all those tentacles and teeth.

James knelt mere yards from where gravel merged with pine straw and hoped he wasn't close enough for a longer tentacle to take his head off. He jammed the mine's limbs between the rocks, plugged in the detonation cord, and scrambled back, unspooling the cable.

If the thing knew what the Claymore was, it betrayed no sign. It kept coming, limbs dragging its bulk along or tearing away limbs and whole trees in its way.

James' back slammed into the warm white metal of a car. He couldn't keep backing away anymore. He was well behind the mine now.

The monster forced its way through the last remaining trees. Sunlight dappled its flesh as crawled onto the gravel. A dozen remaining tentacles rose around it like a swarm of angry cobras. It was all but on top of the Claymore.

James smiled grimly. "Eat this."

He began pumping the trigger.

————

THE CREATURE REARED over the insolent one who'd escaped it days before. Not only had it the gall to avoid becoming food, but then it had come into its lair with the traitor and killed the helpful ones, the ones who gave it living meat. Somehow the boy had even hurt it, tearing away limbs and bursting eyes. The Americans in blue, the "12th Missouri" had hurt it long ago, but only enough to allow a handful to escape. A few hours gorging on the unlucky ones made it as good as new. Whatever the boy had done, it had inflicted far more damage than dozens of men and horses had. The boy had hurt it far more than it had ever been hurt in the long years since it had passed through the cracks in the walls into this world.

This couldn't be permitted. It would eat the boy, eat the girl, and eat the older man with them. Eat them and slink back into the dark waters and heal. It still had eyes and limbs and most of its teeth. Even if the ones who brought it food were dead, it could still hunt. There were deer and the men who pursued them. Those would make fine food. And perhaps even the town the "Americans" had built beyond the borders of its wooded domain. That would be a worthy challenge and a rich source of prey.

But first the boy. It drew back its remaining limbs. Claws flexed. Clawless limbs curled into cudgels. It would punish the insolent worm for daring to hurt it.

But the boy had hurt it somehow when it had charged him. No, it would let the boy *think* it was charging him head-on. Then it would devour him, as it had devoured those "Federals" long ago.

But the boy wasn't afraid. It didn't cry or scream or curse any men or even the creature itself. No, its last words were a cry of defiance.

"Eat this."

The creature threw itself forward and sideways. Whatever the boy had used against it wouldn't hit it in the face, not again...

Before it could turn and hit the boy from the side, thunder cracked. The shockwave struck where its long head merged with its thick torso. With the shockwave came pain. Its skin burned from behind its head down its vast length. Worms of sharp pain burrowed deep into its body. Agony dug through it like a multitude of questing tentacles all burning with the fire of ancient stars.

It reared back away from the blast, bulk rising off the ground. It grabbed for the limbs of the towering pine tree, only for its tendrils to tear away when its great bulk descended. Pain, more pain.

And the agony reached a crescendo when it slammed into the ground.

———

THE EXPLOSION RANG IN JAMES' ears for a long time, all but drowning the police sirens. Though the backblast had washed over him like before, there was no hot metal in it. He drew a breath, nostrils quivering at the smell of smoke, and then opened his eyes.

The sulfurous cloud hung heavily around the mangled bulk of the monster. It lay on its side where the parking lot met the pine straw carpet beneath the trees. A halo of glowing turquoise blood surrounded it, working between the tiny stones. Severed black tentacles writhed in the trees, falling from the upper branches to hang limply off the lower ones or crash to the ground. Wounds holed its side and what would have been its chest looked like a huge piece of Swiss cheese. Glowing azure blood poured out from around pulsing organs. Organs whose pulsing was obviously slowing.

James stood there staring at the monstrosity. A moment passed. Then he laughed. The thing was dead. The thing the rednecks had worshiped out in the woods for God knew how long, the thing that had killed Bill and Sam, the thing whose cultists tried to kill Maad, Dad, Amber, and him, it was *dead*. He laughed again.

"You didn't count on land mines, did you?" he taunted the

dead monster. "You could take bullets just fine, thought that made you so tough. Well, people've got a lot more than bullets now!"

He laughed again.

———

ITS WHOLE BODY was awash in red-hot pain. It was worse around its side, but the blast hadn't spared the rest of it. The world was dark now, submerged in a blackness deeper than its own skin. It hurt so badly it could barely hear the human boy laughing at it.

Laughing. Not screaming in fear and pain or shouting in defiance, but *laughing*. A wave of anger rippled through its huge body. It could feel its lifeblood draining out of ten thousand wounds onto the rough ground below. Centuries spent feasting on the creatures of this world were coming to an end.

But it wouldn't leave this world alone...

———

THE GREAT BULK SHIFTED. JAMES' jaw dropped. The thing had eaten two Claymore blasts and who knew how many gunshots. How it could possibly still be alive?

Maybe human weapons couldn't kill it. Maybe they could hurt it, but no matter how much pain they inflicted, it'd just get up again. It'd keep going and going like some fucking Energizer Squid.

The huge head swung at him, a living cudgel of black flesh slick with blue-green blood. No more evil azure eyes glowed, but it wouldn't need those to swallow him alive. Its huge mouth hinged open, most of its teeth gone but enough left to shred his flesh.

James scrambled back over the hood of the car he'd backed into. The monster tried to roar, but what resulted was more like the world's deepest wheeze. Hot wetness slammed into him, burning again in the wound on his cheek and in several wounds he didn't know he had. He fell onto the other side of the car, desperate to put as much space between himself and the monster as possible.

He needn't have bothered. The enormous head settled onto the ground. It slumped down onto the gravel and lay still. The only movement was from the blood pouring from its array of wounds.

An engine roared behind him. "James!" Dad shouted. "James, we've got the car going! Get in!"

James ignored his father. The thing lay there, turquoise blood spreading through the gravel around it. Could it be dead? It had enough strength for one last attack even after two Claymores.

He stepped around the car toward the monster. His feet carried him around the creature's head toward where its neck would've been. He inhaled. This was insane. He should listen to Dad. He should get the hell out of there.

But he had to be certain. He rushed forward and kicked the shiny black flesh as hard as he could. Though he nearly shouted with pain, nothing happened. He kicked it again with the other foot, not as hard this time. The thing in the woods lay there unresponsive. Unmoving. A corpse.

Then he laughed again. "It's dead!" he shouted. "Dad, Amber it's dead!" He turned toward the cultists' car. They should come out here. They should come see what he'd done!

James soon learned why they stayed put.

Cars topped by spinning blue lights and bearing the dark blue and white of the Edington Police Department spilled into the parking lot, their brakes squealing as they came to a stop.

The noise of the sirens reached an ear-splitting crescendo. Policemen spilled out, handguns drawn and pointed straight at James. Some carried even heavier weapons, assault rifles or what looked like a rocket launcher. As they poured toward him, James caught a glimpse of a man in a dark suit and sunglasses.

It could be worse. They could be from the Sheriff's Office.

Slowly, James raised his hands.

CHAPTER SIXTEEN

"SOMEONE TO SEE YOU NOW," THE LARGE BLACK NURSE said. She stepped out of the room. After a second, an Edington cop came in. He looked vaguely familiar, with cropped blond hair and bright green eyes. Maybe he was the one who'd cuffed him to the fucking hospital bed.

And the man didn't come in alone. Behind him in the doorway was a man in a black suit with a simple golden tie, the one James had gotten a glimpse of when the Edington cops invaded the place of sacrifice. He watched James from behind black sunglasses. James and his hospital bed reflected in the dark lenses; there was no hint of color or feeling behind them. The sight uncomfortably reminded James of the way the thing had looked at him. The man bore no obvious weapon, but James immediately knew he was more dangerous than the policeman.

The cop sat down in the comfortable chair beside James' bed. He handed James a clipboard with a few sheets of paper. "Read them and sign."

James read through the papers, his incredulity growing

with each page. Dad kidnapped by deranged meth addicts who'd broken into the house? He and Sam chasing them on their own? A meth lab guarded by a pet Kodiak bear? *What the hell?* He set the clipboard down on the sheets in front of him.

"That was *not* a bear."

The officer sighed. He leaned forward into James' personal space. James tensed.

"Son," he began. "I'll be straight with you. That wasn't a bear. Nobody around knows just *what* that thing was." James doubted that, but he was smart enough to keep his mouth shut. "Thing is, it's dead now. No need to talk about it anymore."

James sat straight up in the bed. His handcuffs clattered on the railing and bit into his wrist. "No need to talk about it? People *died*! Lots of people!"

The officer scowled. "I flew to New York City to help dig folk out of the rubble. *That* was lots of people. Couldn't have been more than eighteen this afternoon."

Just eighteen? There seemed to be so many. "Deputies from the Sheriff's Office were the first on-scene and ran into Claymores stolen from the National Guard armory. Several, along with some innocent bystanders, were killed in the blast. The EPD provided backup and killed the meth dealers and their trained bear. A nice, neat story. All we need is for you to sign off on it."

It was a nice, neat cover story. All that was necessary was he *lie*. Lie about the *thing* that had killed Sam, killed Bill. Lie about the people who'd tried to kill him and Dad.

Dad. Where was Dad? And where was Amber?

The officer anticipated the question. "Your father's here. The doctors cleared him to leave once we get this sorted out. Same with Amber." The officer leaned forward. "Given her family's history, Amber's been quite cooperative. She's already signed off on the cover story. And your Pa's got some good news for you. He's going to be the new county attorney, pending the next commission meeting, of course. His predecessor was in the wrong place at the wrong time this afternoon. The city and county aren't the same, obviously, but we do talk."

Despite the circumstances, James drew in a breath. Dad had been unemployed for months. The county attorney? That meant they weren't moving back to Buckhead anytime soon. But that also meant his Best Buy paychecks were his again. And maybe he could go to UNC Chapel Hill after all.

On the other hand, that also gave his father a very strong incentive to support the cover story.

"Now, as far as you're concerned, both the mayor and the county chairman believe in a thing called a carrot and another thing called a stick. The carrot is that if you sign this affidavit and repeat that it was a bear when anybody asks, you get your pick of any car the city and county have confiscated from drug dealers. With the meth trade being what it is around here, we've got quite a lot to choose from, and with this new federal anti-drug grant we're getting"—he tilted his head toward the man in the doorway—"we can afford to be generous."

James nearly grinned despite himself. He'd wanted to get rid of the crappy Saab since he first had to drive it and now the officer offered him a new car?

If he were willing to lie, of course. That didn't sit right with him. Not at all. Sam hadn't been killed in some half-assed attack on a bunch of drug dealers. No. Sam had been killed by a goddamn *monster*.

"What's the stick?"

"Well," the officer began. "What exactly *were* you doing out in the woods?" The officer leaned forward into James' face. "Those that died were killed by Claymore mines Sam Dixon stole from the National Guard Armory. Maybe you'd been watching a little too much *Breaking Bad* and decided to corner the local meth market. Sam wasn't the sharpest knife in the drawer, so it wouldn't be that hard to get him on board. It's not like he can defend you, or himself, at the moment." He leaned back. "I doubt you'd find the county jail to your liking, or the state death row if we can make all those murder charges stick."

James swallowed. It wouldn't be that hard for him to end up dead in the Edington jail. A (relatively) rich white kid put in the general population? They'd all want a piece of him, especially if the police dropped some hints. And even if they didn't have him killed, he'd bet a lot of the men there hadn't touched a woman in a long time. He squeezed his buttocks together instinctively, but that wouldn't protect him if some big dude decided he looked pretty.

"And there's your little girlfriend too. Maybe she was involved somehow. That paper she signed can always disappear. And what's his name—Jeff Reed—had to be taken off life support. Left alone too long with a whole mess of brain damage. We could look into that." He shook his head. "Poor Brenda Dixon. Failure to render aid is a pretty hefty charge too, even if it wasn't her who brained Mr. Reed with a brass lamp."

Shit. Not only were they threatening him with jailhouse murder now or execution later and probably ass-rape in between, but they had the same fate in store for Amber and Sam's wife. The way they'd ruthlessly swept the deaths of their brothers in law enforcement under the rug meant they'd do what was needed to silence any uncooperative witnesses.

And there was the man in the doorway. The officer could threaten him with all the torments redneck cops could inflict, but the man in black could be much worse. The man could put him in Guantanamo in a gimp mask.

And there was the car besides. A new car, not that piece of crap Saab...

"And don't think you can get out of this by telling the truth at your trial," the officer continued. "Who'd believe you? Sheriff's deputies offering human sacrifices? A giant man-eating squid?" He shook his head. "The nuthouse down in Milledgeville isn't much better than jail, and that's assuming they decide you're really nuts and not just making it up. Sign the papers."

James swallowed. They had him there. "All right." He paused. "I'll take it." He inhaled, trying to salvage as much pride as possible. "When can I come pick out the car?"

The officer smiled and pulled a business card out of his uniform pocket. "Call me when you're all rested up. We'll pick out a time to tour the lots then."

James took the card and set it on the polished nightstand beside the hospital bed. The officer handed him a clipboard with a pen attached by a string of metal beads and the affidavit attached. James took the pen and set the point to the line where his name went.

He paused. Did he want to lie? Only God knew how many innocent men and women had been offered up to that thing. Most of the cultists were dead, but surely some were still alive. They needed to do hard time for what they'd done, if not get the needle.

"Second thoughts?" the officer asked. "Don't be an idiot."

Damn it. He quickly signed his name and shoved the clipboard and pen back at the officer.

"Fine. You win." The words were poison in his mouth. He'd just defeated a murderous cult and the centuries-old monster it worshiped to save Dad, only to end up at the mercy of some hick cop and an MIB.

The officer smiled. "Thank you kindly. Don't lose that card." He freed James' left hand from the cuffs. The man in black stepped aside to let him pass. He nodded to James before vanishing himself.

Once a decent interval had passed, the nurse returned.

"You look tired. Want me to turn the light out?"

Though they'd doused him with painkillers, he could still feel the countless small wounds the day had left. Maybe a good nap would take the edge off. "Sure."

The nurse clicked off the light, burying the room in shadow and darkness.

———

THEY'D LET HIM, Dad, and Amber out of the hospital the morning after he'd sold his soul for a new car and not getting ass-raped. Amber's family had picked her up. When he and Dad got back, James found an e-mail from the Edington Police Department with a list of the newer confiscated cars waiting for him in his Gmail.

And so it was that a week later, after the first graduation practice, James had begged off going to Zaxby's with Maad, Katie, and Alex. Instead he had Mom drive him to the red brick headquarters of the Edington Police Department. The officer who'd forced the "deal" on him took him to the lot behind the building where two new—to James, at least—cars awaited.

"If I were you, I'd pick that one," the officer said. He pointed a long finger at the silver 2010 Acura sitting closest to the big building's back door. "Paint got a bit scuffed up when we detained the drug dealer it used to belong to." His finger shifted to the cherry-red BMW. "That one's got a better paint job, but its gas mileage isn't as good. Gas won't be a buck fifty a gallon forever."

James nodded. He wanted to get the car and get the hell out of there. And what the officer said about the price of gas made sense.

He pointed to the Acura. "I'll go with that one."

"Good man." The officer stepped over to the car he'd brought James in. While the officer rooted around the glove box, James looked at his prize. It was a damn nice-looking car, and selling the crappy Saab would help cover the insurance on it for a while. He smiled. He'd be rid of that piece of shit car forever now.

Then the sun emerged from behind a cloud. Sunlight glinted on the dark windshield. Just like it had glinted on the waters in the woods where the thing had lurked. His heart began pounding. He swallowed. He was at the Edington police station. He'd survived the monster. He'd killed the monster. He closed his eyes, summoning an image of Amber laughing at one of his jokes. But instead, all that came was the sight of Sam hanging from the monster's tentacles. Hanging just like Bill had. Nausea wrapped around his stomach like one of those tentacles—

"Hey," the officer said, suddenly yanking James back to reality. "You okay?"

James quickly nodded. The officer laid a hand on his shoulder. "Don't worry," he said softly. "This too shall pass." He handed James the clipboard with the ownership papers. Glad to focus on something else, James quickly signed off on everything.

The officer smiled. "The Edington Police Department thanks you for your help. The town is a better place thanks to folks like you." He handed James the rectangular black and silver key fob and set off for the building. James waited for him to disappear inside before he clicked open the car. The Acura still had the new-car smell. He sank down into the driver's seat, enjoying the luxuriant interior. That brought a small smile to his face. He'd barely started sending Mom a text message letting her know he'd be going driving for a while when his phone buzzed. It was Amber.

"Hey there," she said, the smile in her voice lifting his spirits. "What's up?"

James buckled himself in. "Not much." An idea occurred to him. He smiled. "I've got a surprise I'd like to show you."

"What sort of surprise?" There was mischief in her voice now. James smiled.

"If I tell you, then it's not a surprise." He paused. "You want me to come to your place and show you?"

"Sure. You need my address?" That she supplied, one of the better neighborhoods on the east side of town. "How long do you think you'll be?"

"I'm at the..." His voice trailed away. They'd probably offered Amber a similar deal, but no need to remind either of them. "I'm on the west side of town. It won't be more than fifteen."

"Got it. See you then."

James hung up, quickly rewrote his text message, and put the phone away. He habitually pushed the key-fob toward the dashboard before stopping himself. Keyless ignition. Instead, he pressed the button by the steering wheel and was rewarded with the engine rumbling to life. He put the car in drive and rolled out of the police headquarters onto the residential street beyond.

As he pulled onto Fairmont Street and headed east to where Amber lived, the dark thought occurred to him.

There were plenty of places where strange things were reputed to lurk. He'd long written those off as stories, but this one had turned out to be true.

What if there were more?

ABOUT THE AUTHOR

Matthew W. Quinn (b. 1984) grew up in Marietta, Georgia. After graduating from the University of Georgia with a dual degree in magazine journalism and history, he had an extensive career in Atlanta media before moving onto social-studies education. Throughout all of this, he has written science fiction, fantasy, and horror. His first sale was the short horror tale "I am the Wendigo" to the webzine CHIMAERA SERIALS and he later wrote licensed fiction for the BattleTech science fiction universe. 2017 saw the publication of his horror novel THE THING IN THE WOODS, while 2019 saw the publication of his horror-comedy novella LITTLE PEOPLE, BIG GUNS. He is a member of the Atlanta chapter of the Horror Writers Association.

Matthew is also a regular participant in the podcast MYOPIA: DEFEND YOUR CHILDHOOD in which the movies you enjoyed as a child are put on trial to see if they hold up. He can be reached at mquinn1984@gmail.com.

 twitter.com/MatthewWQuinn

ALSO BY MATTHEW W. QUINN

The Atlanta Incursion (Book 2 of *The Long War* series)
Battle for the Wastelands: A Steampunk Military Fantasy
Son of Grendel: A Battle for the Wastelands Novella
Flashing Steel, Flashing Fire: Ten Tales of Valor and Imagination

Made in the USA
Columbia, SC
02 October 2024